Disclaimer

This is a work of fiction. Names, characters, businesses, places, events and incidents are either the products of the author's imagination or used in a fictitious manner. Although it is based around the famous cricket ground there is no official association with the Marylebone Cricket Club (MCC) or Lord's Cricket Ground.

The Mouse Cricket Caper (MCC)
By Mark Trenowden

2019 Edition

ISBN 978-1-5272-3574-8

Illustrations by
Steven Johnson
www.steillustrates.co.uk

Dotball Books
Halifax
Nova Scotia, Canada

www.marktrenowden.com

.

The Mouse Cricket

Caper

Mark Trenowden

BY THE SAME AUTHOR

The Indian Mouse Cricket Caper

The Mystery of the Goodfellowes' Code

The Miracle of Bean's Bullion

Bonzo the Wonder Dog and the Cricket World Cup

Chapter One

The Ashes 2013 Second Test at Lord's
Day One

For Compo, there was no better place in his world. He loved this spot, balanced cross-legged on a globe four stories up. The mouse daydreamed with eyes closed as the warmth of a summer's day seeped out of the city streets and wafted up to meet him. A rising thermal ruffled his tawny brown fur. His whiskers bristled, and his pink nose twitched. A wave of a paw brushed the itch away. He opened his eyes and scanned the landscape before him. Ahead lay an odd assortment of geometric shapes, backlit by a mix of sunset and streetlight. This was the backdrop to Lord's, the world's most famous cricket ground, located on the edge of Marylebone with the West End beyond. Combined with a backing track of the mingled sounds of a London evening, it was truly exhilarating.

Actually, he was balanced on top of a red cricket ball, part of the MCC monogram and cast iron crest at the top of the Lord's Pavilion. The entwined letters sat on top of a tent-shaped turret at one end of the rust-red Victorian building. If Compo had known that over a hundred years before they'd built this place in just six months, he might not have felt so comfortable. What clever chaps they'd been those Victorians creating this iconic building for the cricketing world, with space for a team under each of the turrets standing proud like sets of stumps—a wicket-shaped 'Long Room' between the two. Its symmetry reflected the layout of the game whose soul it housed.

What a great day it had been Compo thought to himself. Throughout it, in the depths of the building, the mouse had bided his time. He'd been able to watch some of the cricket through a hole in the eye of one of the carved terracotta heads that supported the building's terraces. Stone-faced cricketers of the past watching over the passing cricket eras to the modern day. Who'd have thought that behind this unblinking face, there sat a twitching bundle of energy? Secretly drinking in the spectacle whilst waiting for, what in mouse terms, was the main event. A few hours from now, the Lord's hubbub would be gone, and the building would be empty. Until then, patience was needed, as match days brought with them both danger and supplies. Today there would be a bumper harvest.

The first day of a test match was always boom time, and test matches got no bigger than those between England and Australia.

During the day all sorts of activities took place behind the façade of the Lord's Pavilion. To the mice, it was a cacophony of banging, clinking, clapping and cheering. Early in the evening, the noise would die away, and from this they took their lead. As soon as it was safe to venture out, Compo and his friends would break cover, each of the small residents of the Lord's Pavilion scuttling off to complete whatever task they'd been set for the resident colony. Each one had been given a thing to scavenge from a varied list of items that might be lost or discarded. The assortment of things they'd gather would all be put to good use.

The 'Mumbles' were the source of these treasures. Compo knew they were called this because he'd heard a steward who manned the pavilion doors complaining about them. What Compo had in fact heard was the word 'Members', the Members of the Marylebone Cricket Club—a group so varied in their quirks and peculiarities that it would be impossible to define a typical MCC member.

Love of the game bound them all. Similarly,

everyone had a story about how they became a member; the reason for this being that you can't just walk up to Lord's and sign up to be one. Becoming Prime Minister might be one way of jumping the queue. Or playing cricket for England might help things along. For the majority, however, the process was difficult, complicated, and above all, long. Twenty years one might wait to receive the little red passbook and the right to wear the club's red and yellow colours. Of course, once awarded this right, there was no holding them back. Therefore, on match days, it seemed everyone in the pavilion, man or woman, was wearing something red and yellow. Some were quite showy about it whilst others more subtle. The other trait that seemed to go with the territory was to use their visit as an excuse for all-day noshing. There were plenty of places to have a spot of lunch or afternoon tea, but it was the picnickers that the mice were interested in. They tended to have more varied refreshments; things that disintegrated into big crumbs like homemade cake, or dropped and rolled like grapes, nuts and sweets.

On this occasion, Compo wasn't helping to stock the colony's larder; instead, he was on matchstick detail. This was a particularly important commodity in the mice of Lord's world, of which more later. He knew that the best place to find these was on the roof terrace. There was one particular 'Mumble' well known for smoking a distinctive curly pipe who liked to sit up there on match days. Compo's hunch had been right, and sure enough, he'd found a sprinkling of spent matches by one of the wooden armchairs up there.

He'd gathered them up, and having tied them in a neat bundle, slung them across his chest. His job done, he'd made his way up to his favourite vantage point as a reward. It was a tricky climb, but with a building of this age and an intimate knowledge of every nook and cranny, most things were possible. On top of each of the turrets of the Lord's Pavilion is a casting of the Marylebone Cricket Club's emblem. Atop the entwined letters MCC are two red cricket balls, and on top of one of these sat the neatly folded brown furry form of Compo. He was easily recognisable on account of his faded blue cap. He always wore it, wedged between his bluey-pink translucent ears. His Aunty Nesta had made it for him. Designed to look like a real England cap complete with an embroidered badge of three mice topped with a small crown.

The efforts of the evening had tired him out. After

the 'Mumbles' left the building, there was a short period for the mice to get to work before the cleaning staff arrived. During this time, a determined mouse with a mission to perform pretty much had the run of the place. But there again, when you're only 9 centimetres tall, climbing four floors of a building is quite a task. In the sultry early evening air, Compo's eyelids grew heavy, and before long, he was making a high-pitched nasally snoring sound.

'PSST!'

The sound woke him with a start. He looked over his shoulder. How could there be anything there? He was balanced on the very top of the building for goodness sake. He gave his ear a thorough itching with his paw.

'PSST!'

There it was again. Compo pinpointed the source and honed in on it. It appeared to be coming from a gutter below him. He got to his feet, stretched and stepped seemingly into oblivion. In actual fact, in a well-practiced manoeuvre, he had nimbly jumped down from his perch onto the pitched roof below. A short slide brought him up short in the guttering. In the corner of it was a dark hole. He made his way to it and stuck his head down it. Just as he did so, a cry or more of a shrill drawl emanated from the depths below.

'It's teatime, yer flamin' gallah!'

The Aussie twang of Thommo, the only antipodean resident of the Lord's Pavilion, was unmistakable. He was hard at work gathering cherry pips from beneath one of the slated benches on the upper terrace of the pavilion. Thommo had been a resident of the Lord's Pavilion for a couple of months. An Australian Shark Bay mouse, he'd escaped from the nearby London Zoo and decided to do a spot of sightseeing since he was in the area. He'd been welcomed into the Lord's colony despite the traditional rivalry between England and Australia. He was an abrasive character, never short of a sharp comment, but he was well liked.

Compo didn't need telling twice. He was ravenous, and he didn't want to miss out on his share of whatever was on the menu. All that stood between him and some very welcome 'nibbleage' was a death-defying descent and a twisting and tortuous journey.

Beneath him, he had another small roof to negotiate. He travelled down it in a power-slide like a ski jumper. As the edge, a steep drop and his imminent doom became things to worry about, he launched himself into the air. The home team flagpole brought his passage to an abrupt end, and he clung to it star-shaped. From here, the only way was down, and he slid to the bottom, aware that the heat generated by the friction was only just bearable.

Off the pole and onto the balcony he skipped. He scampered where only hours before the television cameras had filmed the England captain rest his chin on his folded arms. Off the balcony, a small hop onto a bench and then down to the floor. A tight squeeze through a gap nibbled in the corner of the door. This was Gatt's handiwork, a mouse endowed with the finest set of incisors in the community. The pavilion handyman was always plugging this up. The amount of squeeze required to get through depended on how this seesawing battle between man and mouse stood. It is a fact that because of their soft skulls, a mouse needs a hole about the size of a penny to pass through. The same could not be said for Compo's collection of matches, and he struggled to push his bundle through lengthways before following it.

Across the deserted home changing room he continued to a hole in the base of one of the green bench seats. He paused a second, looked about him and then vanished. He'd passed into the skeleton of the building.

Here a whole other world existed unseen by the staff and everyday users of the pavilion. A series of well-worn routes cutting this way and that ensured safe passage. A network that had evolved rather than been planned, but one that made Harry Beck's distinctive map of the London Underground look pretty simple.

Compo climbed down a moth-eaten telephone cable long since disused and abandoned. The old, brown, frayed cloth covering of the cable deteriorated with every descent. On this occasion, it held firm, and before long, Compo had dropped from it and was tripping along an old water pipe now disconnected and bent at an alarming angle. He ducked to avoid a nail driven carelessly through a floorboard and felt its unforgiving steel as it scored a line down his back as he squeezed past.

Compo passed through a succession of ramps, cracks, squeezes, falls and diversions. They'd taken him through walls and under floorboards and down a drop of three floors. As he scurried this way and that, a slightly less agile force of nature was making more sedate progress through the building. Once the pavilion had emptied for the day, 'McCrackers' would make his rounds of the building.

James Arthur MacTavish, educated at Eton, captain of Somerset, and in his own words, the unluckiest Scotsman not to have played for England. In his day, he had been a useful right-hand opening bat who if called upon could bowl the odd leg break in an emergency. Forty-five years had passed since those glory days, and now all that remained were his memories and a walking stick fashioned out of an old bat. Two faint green lines, the remains of the bat's logo, bore out McCrackers' claim that it had been given to him by the great all-rounder Gary Sobers. These days, the sound of Sir Garfield hitting sixes had been replaced by the heavy clonk of the bat hitting the floor as it propped up McCrackers.

Compo's route brought him out of a small hole just beneath the Honours Board listing past presidents of the MCC. He stuck his head out into a corridor. Light spilled into it through the double doors that led out to the seating at the front of the pavilion. Blinking away the transition from dark to light, he checked his surroundings. The coast was clear, so he launched himself like a champagne cork, his small bundle trailing in the air behind him. As he landed, he froze for a moment to get his bearings. He cocked his head on one side and listened.

Coming from the depths of the building was the unmistakable wooden clonk that signalled the presence of McCrackers. He, having just answered a call of nature, had passed through the door marked 'Out' next to the one marked 'In' of the gents' washroom—the labels being a sort of cricketing joke. He arrived at the top of the stairs puffing gently. It was no wonder as he was always incredibly overdressed. Today's clothing ensemble centred on the red, pink and green striped jacket of Heartaches Cricket Club. He reached into his breast pocket for his pocket watch and clicked it open. There followed some mental arithmetic before he came to his conclusion.

'I'll just breeze through the Long Room and call it a day,' he murmured in a husky Scottish brogue into a full salt-and-pepper-shaded beard.

Compo watched the old man intently. This was how the mice lived. Latching on to a chance here or a morsel there. Acting on impulse and weighing up the pros and cons of any situation or opportunity. If the old man opened the door to the Long Room, it would make his trip home so much more straightforward. He'd have to pick his moment though. He remained motionless, but alert; any sudden movement might be picked up out of the corner of even an elderly eye.

McCrackers painfully fiddled with the handle, and Compo rocked onto the pads of his front paws and tensed. Then suddenly there was action. The door sighed open, McCrackers took a step and Compo darted for a gap. Through the old man's legs he shot towards one of the room's wooden radiator covers to safety.

However, a professional cricketer's hand-eye coordination is something that mere mortals can only imagine. Even though way past his prime, McCrackers reacted instantly to the mouse's intrusion.

'In the name of the wee man...' he bellowed.

Compo panicked at the outburst and scurried under the radiator cover. Beneath it, out of sight of the Long Room's usual visitors, a hole in the wall led straight into the secret world of the pavilion's mouse colony. However, at each of the end walls of the Long Room there are two radiators, and Compo had just disappeared beneath the wrong one. He came up short, horrified as he realised his error. There was no escape, which meant he either had to stay put or make a break for it.

McCrackers, keen to evict the small intruder, was already warming to his task.

'Come out, you little perisher,' he threatened, thrusting his walking 'bat' at the gap beneath the radiator.

Compo certainly didn't want to be squished, and the old boy was proving pretty feisty given how rickety he'd seemed a few moments before. Hoping to catch him on the hop, the little mouse made a break for it.

The old man, however, was a step ahead of him and stuck out a highly polished and weather-beaten shoe. The mouse, finding his way blocked, hesitated for a moment. It was just a split second, and one that he didn't have. In that time, McCrackers brought down the bat.

The old man had no idea rodents made any noise other than the occasional squeak, but the cry of pain Compo let out as the bat crushed the end of his tail was fluent wherever you were placed in the animal kingdom.

'EEEeeeOOUCH!' the tiny creature bellowed.

McCrackers looked down at his miniscule

adversary in disbelief. For a moment, the two eyeballed each other. Then Compo made to go again. Pinned by the tail, he slithered like a car on a skidpan. The sudden movement made the old man jump, and the pressure on the mouse's tail was released.

Compo wasn't going to make the same mistake again. He took to his heels, zigzagging across the floor to the safety of the other radiator cover.

McCrackers flailed after him, bringing his bat stick down time and time again but without success.

In the darkness beneath the radiator, Compo gathered up his tail and hugged it to him to ease the pain. A tear ran down his nose partly due to the pain, but partly due to the trauma of the near miss he'd just had.

Meanwhile, the old man fumed and clumped about the room cursing the rodent.

'You wait till I speak to the secretary,' he snarled in a pointless rant.

Compo didn't care. He slipped through the hole in the skirting beneath the radiator and descended towards and orange glow below.

Chapter Two

'Excuse me, sir, but may I take a picture of you with my wife?' asked Lenny Pascoe, resident of Brisbane, Australia. The startled octogenarian wearing a red and yellow striped blazer whom he'd asked consented without protest.

'You see, our mates back home would never believe us if we told them that you blokes actually went out dressed like that.'

But it was precisely the fact that 'blokes' did go out dressed in that way that was part of the fun—the sense of occasion and pre-match excitement that anyone visiting Lord's for the first time couldn't help but get caught up in. In through the Grace Gates the spectators poured. Australians delighted to be at the Home of Cricket and full of expectation that their team would pulverise the Pommies.

The end of the day had a different feel. The last twenty overs of the day had produced 30 runs. It was hardly scintillating stuff. The spectators' energy had been drained, and the surroundings mirrored this. The sponsors bunting looked less perky. Free placards proclaiming '4' and '6' and other hand-outs lay discarded on the ground. Flattened blow-up batons and plastic cups trodden flat, the inevitable waste that a large group of humans generates.

It had taken Alfie Sprogett an incredibly long time to decide on how best to spend his pocket money in the Lord's shop. He'd had several false starts where the item selected didn't match the amount in his wallet, much to the irritation of his father. Eventually, he'd struck upon the combination of a pencil sharpener in the shape of the Ashes Urn and a 'cricket ball' lollipop. He'd started sucking the lollipop vigorously as soon as he'd left the shop and dropped it only metres from it.

'Don't pick it up,' his father scolded. 'You don't want it now that it's been on the ground. Nasty sticky thing covered in goodness knows what.'

Alfie, over-tired and over-sugared, instantly burst into tears.

While the other spectators walked past this small drama, one in particular watched it play out intently. Crouched beneath a parked car, nestled into one of the wheels was Spiff. Unblinking eyes, hooked snout and a tear through his right ear, he was unmistakable. His black fur made him almost invisible in the shadows.

His eyes widened at the prize on offer. But it was

oh so risky. Rat and humans didn't go well together at the best of times, and his appearance was bound to cause a fuss if he was spotted. Although the crowd had thinned, there was still a steady trickle passing through the East Gate. The last person through had kicked the lollipop, and it had spun alarmingly. Spiff wanted it intact; it would be so much easier to transport like that rather than as a collection of sticky fragments.

But what was this… a lull in the flow? He could make a run for it. Without hesitation, he reacted and out he darted.

Unfortunately, he'd timed his run to coincide with the exact moment Dot Pickett, wife of the gate attendant, had arrived from the opposite direction with a thermos of tea. As Spiff ran, he skipped over the end of Dot's 'peep-toe' sandals, alerting the wearer to his presence. Dot looked down. For a moment she hesitated, then she tensed. A combination of surprise and disgust at the sight of a black, furry intruder registered in the shrillest of screams.

'RAT!' she cried before spiralling on her heels in a swoon.

An Aussie spectator with a huge walrus moustache caught her on the way down.

'You all right, love?' he enquired, cradling the now gurgling woman in his arms.

'There!' she screamed, pointing a trembling finger.

Spiff had made it to the lollipop, and having taken a firm grip of the stick, he skipped away, vaulting Dot's shin. The peculiar noises that Dot was making on his account caused Spiff to stop in his tracks for a moment. Rattus Rattus and Homo sapiens gazed at each other for an instant. Spiff having the last word by standing on his hind legs and making an aggressive spitting sound. Dot's swoon returned.

Spiff set off again, skipping this way and that between the feet of well-wishers responding to Dot's cry. A retired major had a swing at him with a furled umbrella, and a passing policeman stamped about in his general direction with a size-10 boot. Spiff was far too light on his feet for them, but he'd need his wits about him for the next part of his little outing.

He waited an instant before launching himself from the curb into St John's Wood Road. The road was clear, and he ducked his snout to one side to avoid inhaling the exhaust of a taxi that had just passed. In that instant, instead of checking to see if the other side of the road was clear, he just ran. He suddenly became aware of heat, noise and darkness.

The wheels on the bus go round and round and squash careless rodents unless they are incredibly lucky. Spiff, realising that he'd somehow got away with running straight under a double-decker bus, pressed his tummy to the tarmac. The bus roared over him until clear sky was visible above him. As the Number 139 bus disappeared, Spiff took his chance and dashed to safety.

It would seem unlikely at this point to find a door marked 'Emergency Escape Route', but this is precisely where Spiff was headed. Just a few yards away stood a pair of grey metal doors marked with a blue sign stating just this. Once at it, Spiff squeezed himself between the doors to safety and into a world of darkness.

Although a bleak and inhospitable place, Spiff's refuge provided safe haven for some other residents of St John's Wood. Down in the depths of the Lord's disused or 'ghost' Underground Station lived the local rat population.

Bristles, the leader of the rat colony, was on the disused platform making an inventory of looted provisions. Several rats had recently made it home and were hoping to please him with their finds.

'Show us what you've got then,' he ordered a nervous-looking, juvenile rat called Rags.

'J-j-just this,' he stammered, holding out a bag made out of an old hairnet.

'Let me down, have you?' the older rat threatened.

Bristles turned his head slightly so that he could fully examine its contents with his one remaining eye. Rags shuddered as he saw Bristles' blind eye, the lid sealed with a careless stitch. From the bag he pulled a red and yellow silk handkerchief.

'Oh, but wait now. You have surpassed yourself, young Rags. I like this, I like this a lot.'

Bristles took the handkerchief and fashioned a sort of pirate headdress from it. He pulled one side of it over his blind eye and admired his reflection in a puddle of water.

'Very dapper,' he murmured to himself.

His daydreaming was interrupted by the noisy arrival of two excitable characters: Twitchy and Scruffer.

'Oi, Bristles,' Twitchy blurted out. 'Humans... there are two humans upstairs.'

Normally, Bristles, who was well named given his

prickly nature, would have not taken too kindly to such an interruption. However, there was an understanding within the colony that where safety was concerned, there was no compromise. Whatever, wherever or whenever there was a threat, it was every individual's duty to alert the others without delay.

As a result, no sooner had Twitchy made his announcement than the gathering on the old station platform broke up. Not only did the meeting come to an end, but also the participants vanished instantaneously as if magicked away. In fact, each of the rats had their own particular hidey-hole to take refuge in until the danger had passed.

On this occasion, the rats in the disused station need not have panicked. The two employees of the London Underground were preparing the site for some upcoming works. As a result, they were fixing notices to the various points of entry.

'Here, Bert, hold this while I get my hammer,' said one of the men.

'Oh yeah, when I nod my head, you hit it, that old one,' joked Bert as he held up the notice with outstretched arms.

Evening works
Notice of Pest Control Treatment

The notice read.

'Gawd knows, why we have to put these up. 1939 the last paying customer was down here.'

'It's so we don't go poisoning any wandering hobbits, mate,' his colleague replied, rubbing his chin thoughtfully.

'What are you on about?' asked Bert.

'Elf and safety. Get it?'

The sound of their laughter echoed down the dank stairwells of the old station, causing each of the rats to tense in their various hiding places. Despite any discomfort, there they'd wait for as long as it took for the danger to pass.

Elsewhere, working late in his office, Mr Hobbs, Clerk of Works at Lord's Cricket Ground was on the telephone. The secretary had neatly negotiated the problem he was now handling by ducking it and passing it on. The resulting call with McCrackers was long and rambling. He'd let the old boy wind himself up whilst holding the receiver away from his head. Now he was doing his best to calm him down.

'I understand you've been trying to speak to someone... yes, I had heard... absolutely, I can understand your concern... yes, I'm on top of the situation. I'll keep you posted.'

Actually, this was a tiny white lie aimed at keeping McCrackers off his back. He had 28,000 spectators arriving the next day, and they'd be expecting to find the ground shipshape. The next day's play was his immediate concern, and anyway, McCrackers always had a bee in his bonnet of some description. No doubt it would be something else tomorrow.

He picked up the telephone and dialled again. The telephone that received his call was situated by one of the entrances at the back of the Lord's Pavilion. Normally, this area was manned by at least two of Lord's fiercest 'policemen'—marked out by their beige jackets, that most feared of all Lord's officialdom, the pavilion steward. These steely men and women were specially selected for their roles. They took no nonsense whilst supervising the implementation of the pavilion's strict codes of behaviour and dress. Authorising just the right people to just the right places and laying down the law when required. These enforcers of the rules of cricket watching could, with just a well-chosen word, dismiss the most self-important or argumentative visitor.

But the telephone rang unanswered, its ring frightening the living daylights out of Willow, a pink coloured, female mouse. She'd just stuck her head out of a gap under a window ledge right next to the phone.

Willow had been on the lookout for a particular item, flat wooden ice-lolly sticks. She was very particular about finding just the right ones. She'd reject far more than she'd collect. Running a critical eye over them and then discarding those that didn't come up to scratch. She'd had particular trouble today finding any that would do and had lost track of time. She'd made matters worse by taking a wrong turn in the gap between the floorboards under the 'Away Team' dressing room. She'd squeezed her way through a mess of Victorian lath and plasterwork inside the walls, twisting and turning her way downward. This had brought her out caked in dust by the little writing desk that housed the Pavilion Visitors Book.

She sat for a moment, banged her head on one side to shake the ringing from her ears and then dusted herself down. Her fur changed from pale pink to a light honey colour as she groomed herself. Oblivious to the mess she was making, she took stock of her surroundings. Straight ahead was a flight of stairs down to the basement, and to her right were a couple of steps to an area that on match days was a busy intersection. Wherever she was, she'd have to retrace her steps as the drop to the floor was just too far. She didn't like the idea of risking a fall too much, so she looked about her to weigh up any other options.

On a row of hooks on the wall to her left there was a striped blazer on a hanger.

It belonged to a gentleman who travelled up on match days from Canterbury in Kent. Leaving it in the pavilion saved wear and tear on it and its owner from ridicule.

Willow reckoned that she could use it as a sort of mouse scramble net to get closer to the floor. She steadied herself for a moment and then leapt at the coat. For a moment, she enjoyed the free-fall sensation, then suddenly everything went dark. She'd managed to throw herself into the pocket of the blazer and then fallen through a hole in the bottom of it.

Finding herself trapped, she rushed about the inside of the garment, causing it to come to life, jiggling about on its hanger. The more she thrashed around, the more entangled she became, and eventually she exhausted herself. Tired, worn out and trapped, she burrowed down into the lining and fell asleep.

Chapter Three

'Bye heck, it's about time,' boomed Fred as Compo scampered past, his bundle bouncing behind him.

'Looks like I've just broken another set. Take 'em straight down to yon young'un,' he said in a thick Yorkshire accent, jabbing a thumb over his shoulder.

Fred was standing at the entrance to a makeshift cricket net made from an orange onion bag strung between six pencils pilfered from the 'Members Shop' in the pavilion basement. The whole construction was held in place with a series of string guy ropes pinned to the ground. In it, wearing pads and a hollowed out conker as a helmet, was Knotty. He was attempting to rebuild the stumps, but the middle one had been broken in half.

'Here you go,' said Compo, untying the matches and handing Knotty one.

'Fred's worked up quite a head of speed,' Knotty replied apprehensively, taking the matchstick stump off him. 'He's all worked up because Willow's gone missing, and he wanted her to have a look at his bat.'

'She'll turn up; she's probably just got carried away with her bat search. You know how fussy she is about finding just the right piece of wood.'

'No one's seen her, and now everyone's in a bit of a flap. There's going to be a meeting after mealtime. ' He placed the bails on top of the stumps. 'See you later if I survive this,' he grimaced. 'Okay, Fred, bowl up.'

Compo scuttled away to safety as Fred came careering in off his long run. He bowled the ball, pitching it hallway down the wicket. Knotty did his best to keep his eye on it, but it was too quick for him. At the last minute, he ducked away and the ball flashed past his ear, slamming into the netting.

'Keep your head down, Knotty,' Compo warned as he left the two to their practice.

The space beneath the Long Room that the mice inhabited was naturally divided into a maze of rooms by the floor joists. There had been a colony of mice here for over a hundred years. The pavilion had been completed in 1890, and the mice had moved in soon afterwards. There had been ups and downs to contend with. A period during the Second World War, when first-class cricket was suspended had been a hard time to weather, and the mouse population had dwindled. Above their quarters, the Long Room had been stripped bare. Food was scarce, rations were just that for the entire population, whether you were a mouse or man. Having survived that time, the only other real threat to their wellbeing was in 2004 when the pavilion was refurbished. Then they'd got dangerously close to being evicted permanently—saved by the fact that an annexe of their home was located under the southernmost fireplace in the Long Room and the stone slab set into the floor there.

With the passage of time had come the staining and patina of age. Beneath the floorboards, the oak joists had aged to a deep brown, and between them little trails were worn smooth with the passage of thousands of little feet. Similarly, the edges of openings were worn smooth, rubbed by the furry flanks of mice and their constant comings and goings.

The cricket practice area occupied a main thoroughfare from which branched out a series of rooms, stores and accommodation. Their light source was the glowing suns of the pavilion's security lighting. These were situated on the ceiling beneath their home and burned day and night. There were enough of these lights for the mice to function. With a bit of imagination, the mice had managed to use them to the best effect. Areas that needed to be lit such as the dining area, the nursery and cricket net were, while others like the dormitories and stores weren't.

It was a carefully ordered community with the access to each area maintained by a crew of 'munchinators'. There was no shortage in recruiting volunteers, as all the mice needed to have a good gnaw on things to keep their teeth worn down. From time to time, a member of the Lord's maintenance staff would discover an area. There would be a lot of fuss, the space would be blocked off and measures put in place to make life uncomfortable for the mouse population. But, by and large, they were careful residents. They knew they were on to a good thing, and they wanted to keep it.

Compo tripped down the corridor away from the cricket net. He was keen to get something to eat after his excursion; it was best to get to the canteen before the youngsters. They were starting to wake up now that the sun was going down. There would plenty of activity with waking children, meals being served and general housekeeping. Those that had gone out earlier would be allowed to rest. While they did so, other little groups would be dispatched for further scavenging while others stayed behind to babysit the little ones.

As the children emerged sleepy from their nests, their parents shepherded them down to the canteen. The very capable Mrs Heyhoe supervised things, making sure that the larger mouselets didn't crowd out the small ones. She was strict but had a kindly twinkle in her eye.

What a breakfast they'd lined up for them today. Normally there would be the distribution of food from their stores. Usually there were small servings of sugar, rice, currants, oats and cornflakes. All of these they'd taken little by little from the kitchens. Match days, however, brought more exciting food, and the best thing about it was that it wouldn't keep. This meant that everybody could, within reason, have pretty well as much as they liked. From bread rolls to chocolate cake, fruit to sweets... all of them gathered, dusted down and shared out.

There was one person missing—Willow. She'd normally try to be at the head of the queue to pick up a snack before disappearing into her workshop. Her harvest of new wood would need her undivided attention. Selecting, gluing, trimming and preparing the colony's latest selection of finest handmade cricket bats.

A meeting had been called to discuss her disappearance, and the older mice were assembling in what was referred to as the 'bothy', a communal snug area for meeting and hanging out. Beefy and Don were already there. As the two leaders of the group, they balanced each other. One boisterous, the other more measured. One big and intimidating, the other small and agile, both of them, however the finest cricketers the world beneath the Long Room had ever seen.

Gradually, the space filled with an assortment of characters all eager to get to the bottom of what had happened to Willow. WG, so called because of his tufty beard. Gatt, who liked a slap-up meal anytime, anywhere, and Bumble, who always loved a joke. Thommo, the Australian representative, and Beaky, who always took everything far too seriously. Ranji, who claimed to have come from Delhi but was actually born behind a chip shop in Shepherds Bush. Knotty, Compo, Fred and CMJ, short for Chief Mouse Judge, considered the calmest and wisest although the most absentminded and disorganised of the group. But, when a decision of great pith and moment had to be made, they'd all turn to him.

'Are we all here?' asked Don.

The group murmured that they were.

'So do we know why we're all here?'

'C'mon, Don,' Beefy butted in, clearly losing his patience. 'Yes, we do, and pointing out that we've lost Willow when we all know she's not here isn't going to help find her.'

'This is all getting very worrying,' Beaky said, the lines at the end of his long nose, attributed to his grandpa being a vole, starting to wrinkle.

'Don't you start,' Beefy snapped.

CMJ pointed out that this was getting them nowhere, and Don called the meeting to order.

'Clearly we are all very anxious about Willow, but we must be strong for her now. I have asked everyone who has been out today if they saw her.'

'I saw her this afternoon when we all set off,' Bumble chipped in with a smirk.

'SHUT UP, BUMBLE!' the group cried in unison.

'What are we going to do?' wailed Beaky. 'She might be... might be...'

'Okay, okay,' said Don, gesturing with his front paws as he did so. 'Let's think about this logically. Beaky, I take your point. We are mice living in a human environment, and we all know,' he scanned the group, 'that the k-word is always a possibility.'

Beaky let out a howl.

'Her hunting ground is a dangerous one with all those children stamping around.' Beefy was right. Not only this, but the ice cream cart opposite the Lord's Museum took her outside the relative safety of the pavilion.

'But you can get ice cream in the Long Room Bar, all those old folks love it... mmm... mmm,' said Bumble, making a sound and pulling a face so that it looked as though he had lost all his teeth.

'Well, if I know Willow, I'm guessing she wouldn't go outside alone,' Don said thoughtfully.

'I agree,' said Beefy. 'And there are plenty of cupboards behind the bar that she could have got stuck in. I'm sure there's a perfectly simple explanation and that she'll be fine.'

'I hope you're right,' wailed Beaky.

'So I suggest we send out a search party. Do I have any volunteers?'

Everyone put their hands in the air, and Don smiled to himself as he surveyed the group. They were weak individually, but they made a strong team.

Later that evening, a little way down the road from the Grace Gates, a couple of vans were pulling into the kerb. They'd parked outside the 'Emergency Escape Route' to the abandoned Lord's Underground Station. Out of each of the vehicles stepped two men wearing white coveralls and headlamps. The cones of their headlamp beams swept round the empty London street. It was as if they were in an old sci-fi film blasting away anything they looked at.

'This is the way in,' said the lead spaceman, turning and illuminating his colleague and the words 'Pest Arrest' on his hard hat.

'I thought we were going to an old tube station,' one of his sidekicks queried.

'It is, but we're going in through the back. The surface building was demolished in the sixties. There's not a lot of it left now. Just thirty-five steps down and a bit of platform.'

'So what's all the fuss about?'

'There's a hotel right next door, and they're not too fond of their little furry neighbours. Not only that, but the rats freak out the track workers who use it for access.'

'I don't like them either—I hate this job,' the third

man, whose coveralls were stamped 'Trainee', shivered and chipped in.

'Aw diddums...' the foreman chastised him unsympathetically. 'Make yourself useful and help get the kit.'

This was the sort of job that had no room for sentiment. The more hardened team members took no prisoners, and while their disgruntled colleague clumped off, they turned their attention to the job in hand. Opening the emergency entrance door made a horrible metallic scraping sound.

Just inside it, Stinger was engrossed in grooming himself. He was very particular about his appearance and liked to keep his fur nice and shiny. Vanity might have been one of his foibles, but he was stationed where he was for a reason.

The sudden movement and noise acted like a starter's pistol. Without a moment's hesitation and with no consideration to his own welfare, Stinger hurled himself down the stairs to alert the others. A sharp turn to the right gave him a bit of trouble, and he cornered on two legs like a cartoon car banking with its wheels in the air. At the bottom of the steps, a group of young rats were playing a knockabout game of football.

'Scarper!' Stinger hissed, and in a moment they vanished, their ball left rolling idly on the empty platform.

Stinger continued his progress.

'Humans in the building—pass it on!' he urged as he ran this way and that amongst the rats nests hidden in the various nooks and crannies of the station. As the last scaly tail whipped out of sight, a silence descended on the old platform.

So the rat community went 'dark' as James Bond would say. They would not communicate from now on to protect themselves. Instead, they watched as the men from 'Pest Arrest' systematically made their home and the surrounding area a minefield of traps and poisons.

Two hours later, the deed was almost done.

'Right, that just leaves the fumigation process and we're outta here,' the foreman announced with an air of finality.

'Ooh, I love this bit,' said the trainee.

'You keep well away from these, young fellow-me-lad, only a fully trained operative can light a rodent smoke bomb.'

The trainee gathered up several of the firework like bombs and helped set them at intervals around the disused station platform. Once they were all in place, the four men put on respirator masks before the leader of the group lit each of the bombs. After a brief flare, the bombs started to belch green, acrid smoke, and the men left them to do their work.

The rat population watched the smoke billow around the platform mesmerised. It was as if a spell had been cast over them, complete with visual effects.

Bristles was the first to realise that the deadly cloud would finish them all if they didn't act quickly. He left his hiding place and let out a piercing shriek. In no time, Twitchy, Bitesize, Stinger, Spiff and Long Tail joined him.

'We've got to get everybody out!' he exclaimed breathlessly.

As he spoke, the shadowy forms of the various families housed in the station were coming out of their hiding places.

'We need to gather everybody and then escort them out of here. We'll take them down the line. It's the quickest way,' he spoke quickly and incisively.

'But surely we can't...' Twitchy had a feeling his

observation wasn't required.

'I know it's dangerous, but we have to go. I'll stay on the platform until the last one's out. Spiff, you head off down the line and clear the 'chute'. The rest of you, space yourselves at intervals along the track. Make sure everybody keeps well into the side.'

Spiff bounded off to clear the entrance to the 'chute'. It was a broken pipe the rats had camouflaged as an escape route that would take them up to street level in an emergency.

So the evacuation began, parents shepherding little ones down onto the covered track, then directing them away from the station. One by one, they assembled and began their escape. A furry line snaked its way down the line, undulating as it passed over the sleepers supporting the rails. The stones that lined the track gave way as they passed over them, causing them to slip so hampering their progress. Not only this, but they were sharp on the little one's feet, making them squeak and protest. There was nothing the elder ones could do but chivvy them along. They didn't want to instil panic in the group, but all the adults were painfully aware that this was a life or death situation.

'Come along, not far to go,' Long Tail urged, giving

everyone that passed a gentle shove to keep them moving along.

Twitchy, however, had spotted a new hazard. Down the track, two headlights pierced the darkness of the tunnel.

'Everyone keep calm!' he yelled. 'TRAIN!'

The message passed down the line. The rats didn't need telling twice. They pressed themselves against whatever there was to press themselves against and waited.

At first there was a barely noticeable tremble beneath their paws, building as the underground train got closer. The lights starting to light the startled faces of the little ones, then suddenly the rushing, roaring, rumbling noise as the train bore down on them. As it arrived, it brought with it an oily, shrieking wind that washed over them. A maelstrom that no sooner had it arrived passed as the train carried on down the track and away from them. The quiet that returned was broken by the mewling cries of the children and ssh-shushing of the parents trying to calm them.

Twitchy ran back and forth up the line urging all the members of the colony to safety. He looked back to see the smoke now billowing over the edge of the platform. Out of it a heavy form fell and landed next to the track. He sprinted back down and found Bristles gasping for breath, his single eyeball rolling wildly. He'd stayed to the last possible moment to ensure that everyone had got away safely. Twitchy grabbed him by the scruff of the neck and dragged him for all he was worth until they were clear of the station.

'Bristles… Bristles!' he cried. 'Stay with me, mate!'

Bristles let out a gurgle.

Twitchy looked about him. There was a half-crushed discarded water bottle lying by the track. He grabbed it and saw that it still had a little water in it. He set to work on one side of it, gnawing for all he was worth. Eventually he pierced the plastic and held the bottle over Bristles so that he could have a drink. It did the trick, and he staggered to his feet, coughing with eyes and nose streaming.

'Did the others get away?' he gasped.

'Yes, they must all be safely in the 'chute' by now. Are you strong enough to make it?'

'What do you think?' he grinned, a gleam returning to his eye.

The two rats scampered off to join the others. They found them waiting in the 'chute.' There was a bit of a bottleneck, and the two rats eased their way through the waiting group.

Everyone was anxious, and at first there was a flurry of questions about what was going to become of them.

'I understand your concern,' Bristles spoke up. 'For now, we'll make our way up to the surface, and then we'll head over to the storm drain in Oak Tree Road.'

The rats had a contingency plan for disasters, but the storm drain was a short-term fix. The road was just opposite the Lord's East Gate, and two blocks of apartments stood at the end of it. Despite the dubious fact that in London you're only ever a few metres from a rat, this could not be a permanent home. The delicate residents of this area would be on their case in a heartbeat.

The storm drain provided some relief, but it was cold an unwelcoming. There were none of the comforts of their normal home. Instead, they had to rely on each other for cushioning, comfort and security. Bristles surveyed his relocated colony. What a night it had been. The children had taken an age to settle, and even now there was the odd squeak. The senior males would have to find a more permanent home, but for now, they were just happy to be safe. That could wait until morning.

Chapter Four

The Ashes 2013 Second Test at Lord's
England 287 for 7 overnight

Some of the MCC members had been queuing since five o'clock in the morning. The chief executive had offered to open the gates early to accommodate some of the older gentlemen. They'd declined, saying that they were happy to wait. It was a tradition they said, and so there they stayed where they were until nine o'clock.

Inside the ground beneath the Long Room floor, the dull roar of the entire mouse population sleeping might have been deafening had there not been intense activity above them.

Passing through the Long Room inches above them were a varied assortment of people vital to the smooth running of a day's international cricket. Their varied assortment of footwear made a weird cacophony of sounds. Squeaks, clip-clopping, scraping on, sticking to and the hard to define ripping sound of pimpled cricket shoes on the lino floor. TV company girls, radio commentators, past England captains now pundits all making their way through the pavilion. Out through the central double doors and down a flight of steps to stake out a place on the playing area. Advertisers, executives, managers of this and that making sure that their business was being done. The umpires had a wander around, looking inconspicuous without their white coats and hats. Add to this mix several cameramen, sound technicians playing out lengths of cable, groundsmen, coaches, medical staff and even the odd cricketer.

Some were kitted out in their training outfits with all their protective gear on the outside. Others dragged wheelie bags of equipment across the outfield to the practice area on the Nursery Ground. A coach with a shortened bat gave high catches while another supervised a fast bowler bowling at a single orange rubber stump. It was a schoolboys' autograph heaven if they could get anywhere near them.

As the gates were opened, the members of the public filtered in to observe this peculiar spectacle. Those with the treasured little MCC red book, however, were eagerly trying to gain access to the pavilion though one of the two rear entrances, each of the members bubbling with restrained excitement that no amount of past visits could diminish. What a treat to be in the pavilion on a day like today with its buzz of expectancy in the air. Today might be a day recorded forever in the annals of cricketing history, and for a lucky few, an opportunity to say that 'I was in the pavilion on that day.'

Once you've made it into the Long Room, the magic is revealed. If you're a cricket enthusiast, you're in heaven. One moment you might almost brush shoulders with the captain of Australia as he takes the field. Of course, all the time, assuming an air that it is the most normal thing in the world. Or another passing England's second highest wicket taker on the stairs pretending to be casual while resisting the urge to say 'Morning, Jimmy.' These are the type of rare treats that the MCC members enjoy. Seeing all this at first hand from the most sought-after spot in the whole of the cricketing world.

What a shame the mouselets were missing it. They'd exhausted themselves mimicking the efforts of the professionals through the night. In their games, their favourite players had not been nicked out for just a few runs. The hundred scored had been made in successive boundaries and the crowd's adoration acknowledged with a wave of their bat. Finally, they'd been packed off to bed to dream of new future triumphs and being selected to play for England.

The adults were exhausted too. They'd been out looking for Willow—search parties sent all over the pavilion to look. CMJ had seen to it that they'd been thorough too. He'd drawn up a list of potential locations and dispatched the mice in pairs to all parts of the pavilion. The Committee Room, both the 'home' and 'away' dressing rooms, the Writing Room, the shop and the Members' Bar. They'd searched the dining rooms, the basement washrooms, every conceivable storage cupboard and all manner of hidey-holes. It was a super mouse effort, but through the night the separate search parties had returned with only bad news.

Reggie Balding's day had started at much the same time as the mice had given up their effort. A taxi had picked him up at his home just behind the cathedral in Canterbury. He'd made the 5.59 a.m. train by a whisker and then had a pleasant catnap on the hour-and-a-half journey into Waterloo East. A wheezing, five-minute descent down several flights of stairs and an escalator had got him onto a Jubilee line train. When he'd emerged from St John's Wood tube station, it was just after eight o'clock, and he felt as if he'd run a marathon.

Starting the walk down the Wellington Road towards the ground, he was joined by some familiar faces. Their chat made the reasonably long walk for the elderly Reggie more bearable. He'd been relieved not to have to stand for too long outside the ground. Soon he was making his way in through the pavilion's north entrance.

'Morning, Mr Balding,' the steward on the door duty welcomed him. 'Wait just a jiffy, and I'll get your blazer for you.' Soon he was helping the old man out of a battered anorak and into the red and yellow striped blazer they kept for him.

Reggie said his 'thank yous' and made his way to the usual seat that had been reserved for him.

Finally in position, just to one side of the steps leading from the pavilion to the playing surface, at last he could relax. That is until the whole process started again in the evening. To celebrate, he unwrapped a bloater paste sandwich. A nearby spectator wrinkled his nose as the fishy smell wafted around. Unabashed, Reggie took a bite, which coincided with an attempt by

Willow to make a bid for freedom. She'd been woken some time before and was now doing her utmost to escape from Reggie's pocket.

'What the dickens is that?' Reggie exclaimed. The old man felt in his pocket, and as his hand found the warm little furry body, his face was a picture of surprise. Normally such a discovery would have drawn a more demonstrative response, but for Reggie Balding, long-time host of children's TV favourite 'Animal Characters', it was no big deal.

Carefully, he lifted Willow out of his pocket and held her on his palm in front of his nose.

Willow, taken aback by this sudden change in her fortunes, could do nothing but sit and look back at the kindly old gentleman. Reggie held up his sandwich, and Willow, who was famished, gave it a tentative sniff before gratefully biting off a fragment.

'Now young err... lady,' Reggie said knowledgeably, 'there are some people round here who won't take too kindly to your presence.' With that, he cupped her in his hands and made off in the direction of the Coronation Garden by the Museum.

McCrackers was at the pavilion entrance fussing about the fact that he'd knocked the head off his match-day carnation. The sight of a fellow old hand distracted him, however.

'Ahh... morning, Reggie. Uneventful trip this morning I hope.'

'Morning, yes, quite straightforward, thanks.' Reggie acknowledged his friend by raising his cupped hands in greeting. As he did so, Willow popped her head out from between his thumbs and then in almost the same instant ducked back down again.

'Did you see that?' McCrackers exclaimed.

'See what?' Reggie replied innocently, hurrying past his friend and out through the doors. 'I'll catch up with you later, old boy. Things to do, people to see.'

McCrackers watched him disappear.

'See that, did you?' he asked of the steward.

'See what, sir?'

'That damned mouse; it nearly did for me yesterday, and here it is large as life again today. Can I use the house phone? I need to speak to the secretary.'

A few hundred yards away, the rats' search for a new home had begun in earnest. The territory they felt comfortable in was just to the south of Lord's. It stretched from the Northern bank of Regent's Canal to the southern side of St John's Wood Road.

On the other side of the road, the sandy brick wall that ran round Lord's contained a world that they had not ventured into. They'd benefitted from the people that visited it and what they left behind, but the wall repelled them like a force field, and they concentrated their search on the area they knew.

Bristles had called a meeting to discuss a list of potential locations. He'd scratched out a rough map of the area on the dusty floor of the drain. Sun spilled through the grating, complicating the lines he'd drawn.

'So this is the canal?' asked Scruffer, pointing at a thick shadow running across the plan.

'No,' Bristles sighed, exasperation in his voice. 'Look, we are here, and the canal is there.' He stabbed a finger in the dust.

'We don't want to go anywhere near the canal,' Mr Cheese, a humourless big black rat, said ominously. 'It is certainly not a good idea with the 'Camden Creature' on the loose. I've heard people talking about the 'Camden Creature', and do you know what it eats? Ratsss.' He hissed the last syllable.

'Thanks for your contribution,' Bristles snapped, barely concealing his annoyance at this unhelpful distraction. Mr Cheese was in fact right. The local newspaper's billboard confirmed various sightings of Aesculapian snakes in the canal, and their diet did include rats.

'What about looking in that huge place with all the pipes on the outside?' suggested Bitesize whilst cleaning the gap between his two front teeth with a splinter of wood.

'Too dangerous,' Mr Cheese chipped in again.

'WhYY?' Bristles queried his voice rising in disbelief.

'Have you heard that humming noise that comes from it? It is electricity, a lot of electricity. If we snoop around that place, there is a very good chance that one of us will be killed. Also, if you stay near it for a long time, it makes your head hurt.'

Mr Cheese was spot on again. The building in question was the St John's Wood electrical substation, part of the area's electrical generation and distribution system. It was perhaps not the best place to try and raise future generations.

'Anyone else got any ideas?'

'There's the scrap yard,' suggested Twitchy.

'Good, now we're getting somewhere,' Bristles said thoughtfully.

'And the church,' ventured Spiff.

'C'mon, boys, we rats have got a bad enough reputation without sniffing around a church,' Bristles scolded.

'What about the fish and chip shop?' Stinger added.

'I like your thinking, Stinger, but too small, and the owner is particularly feisty. He'd chop us into small pieces if he found us,' Bristles counselled.

Mr Cheese, unsmiling, drew a claw across his throat, his gesture indicating that such a move would be close to suicide.

'Enough!' Bristles reprimanded him. 'If you haven't got anything constructive to say, just shut up.'

'I didn't say a word,' Mr Cheese sneered.

Bristles had had enough. He flew at the rat, pinning him to the ground spitting and snarling.

Twitchy and Scruffer reacted almost as swiftly, restraining their leader before he did something he might have regretted later. It had the desired effect, though. As they pulled Bristles away, Mr Cheese struggled to his feet and looked suitably reprimanded.

'My apologies,' he said solemnly.

In the hierarchical world of the rats, showing a little muscle was sometimes a good thing, reminding some of those who needed it just who <u>was</u> the boss. Bristles picked himself up and smoothed the fur down on the back of his neck.

'Now is not the time for petty differences to get in the way of what is best for us all. I suggest as the strongest members of the group, we all have a scout around and report our findings later today.'

For the first time in the meeting, everyone was of the same opinion, and soon the rats were furtively leaving the drain through the grating. Spotty and Skunky, two young males on the edge of the group, had paired up. Each of them had acquired their names on account of the unusual fur markings. Skunky had a broad white line down his black back, and Spotty really needed no explanation. They skipped along the St John's Wood Road, scuttling from one piece of cover to another. The affluent leafy area was actually a real haven for them. In London in certain areas, the life of a rat could be very grim indeed.

The two rats were keen to make an impact amongst the other males, or bucks. To do this, they'd have to come up with something totally off the rats' usual radar. Sadly, they were headed in the wrong direction. Had they gone the other way, they might have come across the ideal solution, a peaceful garden area that they could make their own. That would have really given them some credibility. But what they didn't know couldn't harm them, and they pressed on.

A hold up in the traffic gave them an opportunity to cross the road. Their appearance as they made it to the pavement on the other side caused a flurry of excitement among those having coffee outside the Lord's Tavern. But they continued cheekily on their way. No sooner had they negotiated that potential hazard than the proprietor of the local newspaper kiosk did a curious dance in front of them. This in fact was the symptom of a panic attack brought on by the sudden aggravation of his musophobia, or fear of rats. Neither of the rats could tell whether he meant them any harm, but they gave him a neat sidestep. Just beside the green kiosk was a raised brick flowerbed. The two rats left the ground simultaneously like steeple chasers and found welcome shelter in the bushes. Once hidden from view, the intrepid pair sped on through the foliage.

The flowerbed curved round a corner, taking them into Grove End Road and a noticeable change in atmosphere. They were in a residential street, and the first building they came to was a block of flats. Its whitewashed concrete looked uninviting and impregnable. They carried on. Beyond it, they came to the first of a number of smart-looking family homes. The first had unwelcoming big black-painted gates, but the second looked more promising, and the rats stopped.

'What do you think?' Spotty asked breathlessly.

'Definitely worth a look,' replied Skunky, hopping through the bars of the wrought iron gate. Through the gate was a stretch of drive leading to the house and a small lawn. The sun was now high in the sky, but a tall tree provided some shade. One moment the two rats had been in the middle of London traffic, now they found themselves in an oasis of calm. Skunky padded over to the grass and gave it a prod. The smell of summer rose met his nose and, taken by the moment, he let down his street-wise defences. For a few blissful seconds, he rolled himself on the grass in the sun.

Spotty was taken aback by Skunky's recklessness, but seeing the delight on his friend's face, in a matter of moments he was trying it out too.

Inside the house, Eleanor Merryweather was fussing about her hallway. She'd had the car keys a moment ago, but got distracted and put them down. Ernie the Jack Russell was getting agitated. Seconds before he was going out for a ride in the car, now he was trapped inside. Suddenly the keys miraculously reappeared and the trip was on again.

Mrs Merryweather struggled with the front door. Ernie shivered with frustration and then... the door was open. Ernie burst into the garden, barking with delight.

The rats meanwhile, were oblivious to his arrival and the potential threat he posed.

Having done a circuit of the car, Ernie stopped to wait for his owner. In that moment, he spotted the two rats on the lawn—correction, on *his* lawn.

At this point, Ernie must have taken a deep breath because the sustained burst of ferocious barking he uttered would have required it. If they hadn't noticed him before, the rats jolly well did now. Ernie launched himself in their direction and was homing in like an Exocet missile.

The two rats grabbed each other and clung together for a moment. Then just as Ernie bore down on them, they sprang apart. The two rats had split up, but reconvened under the middle of the Merryweather family car. Ernie took up the hunt again with a renewed burst of bow-wow-wowing.

The rats split up again, but Ernie had formulated a plan. As Spotty made for the gate, Ernie gave chase. Skunky, meanwhile, had headed in the opposite direction and straight into Mrs Merryweather. Her resulting scream distracted Ernie just long enough for Spotty to jag to the left and use the foot of the tree to bank round and change direction. The two rats met at the side of the house, but there was no time to exchange pleasantries. The two were at a full-out sprint.

Ernie was now back on the hunt and bearing down on them. At the back of the house an expanse of lawn stretched ahead of them, and at the end of that a sandy brick wall.

The lawn seemed endless, and Ernie supercharged. He was eating up the ground between them. The rats zigzagged to and fro, which bought them precious yards, and then when all seemed lost, a means of escape presented itself. In the middle of the wall was a green-painted wooden door partly masked with overgrown ivy. The gap beneath it was never going to accommodate a Jack Russell, but there was ample space for a couple of skinny rats. With millimetres to spare and Ernie just a hairsbreadth away, the two rats squeezed under the gate.

Ernie's snout appeared under the gate snuffling this way and that, his once wet nose now caked in dust. The rats paid him no attention as they had unknowingly given themselves another problem. They'd barged into a group of people—to them what seemed like a lot of people. They were in the Lord's Coronation Garden with just the cover of a few thin rose bushes. The two rats did not communicate; they both just stood stock still their chests heaving.

In fact, the people were a group of students hired for the five days of the test match who were manning a champagne stand. The garden was actually pretty quiet for this time of day.

At the same time Reggie wandered into it with Willow still cupped in his hands. He gave the students a friendly nod. They were too engrossed in their mobile phones and conversations to pay him any attention. Soon the garden would be thronging with picnickers and friends meeting up, and they'd be busy. Reggie made his way to the far side of the garden and sat down on a low stone wall. He gently lowered his hands and let Willow go in the flowerbed beside him.

'Off you go, little girl, and take care,' he said.

Willow stepped tentatively from the old man's hands, and then scurried away without looking back. The flowerbed had a wall to one side, and she kept well into it to avoid any further detection. Behind it Ernie had given up his chase in disgust and was trotting back to find his owner. A few feet farther along it, the two rats were still holding their ground when Willow ran smack into them.

Chapter Five

The Ashes 2013 Second Test at Lord's
England 361 all out – Australia 42/1 at lunch

Having been on the back foot up until moments ago, the rats were delighted with their sudden change of fortune. Here was someone that they could bully as they just had been.

'Hello, sweetheart. What can we do for you?' asked Spotty in a menacing way.

Willow's momentary relief at gaining her freedom now turned to despair. She tried to escape, but Skunky was too quick for her and blocked her way. The mouse reared on her hind legs and raised a hand to defend herself. Skunky grabbed hold of it.

'Not so fast,' he warned.

'Ow, you're hurting me,' Willow whined.

'Oh dear, I am sorry,' he said sarcastically, leaning in towards her.

Willow got a good look at his two sets of sharp yellow incisors and wrinkled her nose at the smell of his breath.

'How about a little kiss, gorgeous?' he goaded her.

'Let me go!' Willow insisted, trying to scrabble away from him.

'All right, that's enough, Skunky,' Spotty cut in. 'Let's see if this little lady can help us with what we're looking for. Where have you come from, lovey?'

Willow motioned over her shoulder, but checked herself.

'N-n-nowhere,' she answered.

'Well, if you've nowhere to go, then you might as well come with us,' Skunky smirked.

'No, wait,' said Spotty. 'What was that you were going to say?'

'Hold up,' Skunky interrupted, 'it's starting to get busy here.'

Inside the ground, England had struck on the fourth ball of the last over before lunch. There had been a moment's hesitation to see if they'd complete the over, and then the teams had trudged off. The mass departure from the pavilion was slightly delayed as people liked to see the teams walk back through the Long Room. Now that little bit of theatre had been played out, the pavilion was starting to empty. Many of the spectators were making their way to the garden to be reunited with their picnics left on benches or the patchwork of coloured rugs laid on the lawn.

'C'mon you,' Skunky said, gruffly dragging Willow behind a great big red wheelie bin.

'Where are you taking me?' the mouse wailed.

'If you won't tell us where you live, perhaps you'll tell our guv'nor?'

'Do you think that's a good idea?' Spotty enquired tentatively. 'Aren't we supposed to be solving a problem, not adding to it?'

'Look at her, Spotty. Bright-eyed, clean, well fed. This little cutie is being well looked after somewhere. If she won't tell us where, then perhaps someone who is a bit more intimidating will get it out of her.'

With that, the rats bullied the little mouse further away from the world she knew.

Inside the pavilion, the corridor outside the Writing Room was busy. On several TV monitors there were details of other matches being played that day. The teams for three T20 games blinked out at the passers-by. Some hovered to examine the felt pin board. On this were notices about the various MCC societies, backgammon, tennis, bridge and golf. Add to this people coming in from the seating at the front of the pavilion and others edging out of the Writing Room.

The side door of the Long Room provided another source of bodies. Therefore, the fact that the secretary should encounter McCrackers in all this was an occurrence of incredibly random bad luck.

In the crush, the two men found themselves pressed against each other at extremely unlikely and uncomfortably close quarters.

'He had it in his hands, I tell you. Yes, a mouse in his hands,' McCrackers exploded without introduction.

'Yes, thanks, I got your message about the mouse. I've spoken to Mr Hobbs, and everything is in hand.'

'No, today, here, now. I've just seen it, for goodness sake. A mouse, damn it!' He flapped his hands either side of his head like big ears.

'I understand your concern, absolutely. We're on top of it, I assure you. I'm really sorry, but the Australian team manager is expecting me,' the secretary called back apologetically, allowing himself to be swept away by the tide of people.

McCrackers fumed for a moment and then decided to console himself with a spot of lunch. He planted his bat stick firmly on the ground and made off in the direction of the Long Room Bar. Mr Hobbs, the clerk of works, had just made his way into the pavilion and walked straight into him. He was escorting a curious-looking individual in a big black hat and dark glasses.

'Enjoying the cricket?' Mr Hobbs ventured.

'Yes, useful runs from Broad and Swann,' McCrackers replied, but he was distracted. He eyed Mr Hobbs' companion warily.

'Is this gentleman a member?'

'This is the Pest… er… Mr Pest… er… son,' Mr Hobbs replied awkwardly.

'Peterson,' the man jumped in and corrected.

'Only members allowed in the pavilion on match day,' McCrackers ranted.

Mr Hobbs leaned into McCrackers and said in a hushed tone, 'He's here about the situation.'

'Situation?'

Mr Hobbs raised his eyebrows and nodded in the direction of the Long Room.

'The situation you alerted us to.'

It suddenly dawned on McCrackers what he was on about.

'Ahh, righto. Mum's the word,' he said, tapping the side of his nose with a finger. 'I'll leave you two gents to it then.'

McCrackers disappeared into the Long Room Bar

and Mr Hobbs showed Bob, the Pest Arrest representative, into the Long Room.

'When I said come in disguise I hadn't quite pictured this,' Mr Hobbs said to his guest.

'Is it too much?'

'Well, perhaps a little, I think you can lose the hat and the glasses. I just meant not to come in overalls emblazoned with the words 'Mouse Killer'.' Mr Hobbs enjoyed his own joke for a moment, then reeled in horror.

Ashton Agar, the Australian who had scored 98 on his test debut, was just walking through the Long Room having had a practice net on the Nursery Ground. Bob, not knowing the pavilion etiquette regarding autograph hunting and picture taking, stepped into his path, his camera phone to his eye.

Mr Hobbs pulled him to one side.

'Please, no photographs in the pavilion,' he said sharply.

'All right, keep your hair on. I was just getting a picture for my nephew.'

'Well, please don't,' Mr Hobbs ordered.

They carried on and walked the length of the Long Room to where McCrackers had reported his sighting.

Mr Hobbs looked about him to check that no one could overhear him.

'It seems that the point of entry is behind these radiator covers. Obviously, when you return this evening, you'll be able to take these off.'

Bob pulled a screwdriver from his inside pocket, bent down and prodded about beneath the radiator cover.

'Now, regarding the method of dispatch,' Mr Hobbs said, leaning over the technician's shoulder.

'Eh?'

'How are you going to sort out our little problem?'

'Well, there are a number of methods, but my particular favourite is the MILK.'

'MILK?' Mr Hobbs said quizzically.

'Mouse Instant Lethal Killer,' Bob said knowledgeably. 'It's brand new on the market, a state-of-the-art, humane trap. Even sends you a text when you've got one of the little critters.'

'My goodness, that is high tech. How many will it take at a time?'

'Just the one, in they go, a little blast of inert gas, and bye bye, mousey.'

'Only one? That won't do at all. If we have a family

in residence, then I'm afraid they all have to go.'

'Well, then there's yer poison. But that causes NIFs.'

'NIFs?' Mr Hobbs enquired.

'Nasty Invasive Fumes. That's dead mouse pong to you and me.'

'Shush, not so loud,' Mr Hobbs insisted, once again checking about him. 'I will leave it to you. Do whatever you have to do, but get rid of them. I'll see you later on this evening.'

'No problem, all I need now is the exit.'

'EXIT?' Mr Hobbs questioned. 'What does that stand for?'

'Err... the way out, mate.'

Bob's clonking about had woken some of the adult mice. Don wasn't sleeping well anyway and had left his bed to sit in Willow's workshop. At sometime over the years, a chock of wood had been wedged in as an extra support for the floor above. This made the space too tight for general activity, but perfect as a cubby-hole for Willow. Propped up along the walls were cricket bats in various stages of construction or repair. A heap of ice cream lolly sticks waiting to be glued and trimmed. Rubber bands dropped by the postman for handle grips. Most importantly, Willow's range of tools, little wood planes and draw-knives made out of razor blades. The player's changing room was a good source for these. Her apron lay next to a pot of flour and sugar glue and a ball of string salvaged from any number of different places.

All of these items lay sadly as she'd left them as a shrine to Willow. There was a hole in the ceiling below Willow's workshop that let in more light than anywhere else in their underground lodgings. She plugged it with an old cork when not working, but Don had pulled it out to look about the space. Light spilled into the main corridor, and as the mice that had been woken got up, they were drawn to it. Soon there was a collection of them. Quietly they assembled and formed a circle round Willow's stained and scarred workbench. Beefy, Don, WG, Gatt, Bumble, Thommo, Ranji, Knotty, Compo, Fred, Beaky and CMJ. Each of the mice put a hand on the other's shoulder, and they formed a circular huddle as the cricket teams who played above them did. There they stood in silent reflection, grieving for the loss of their co-worker and friend.

Chapter Six

The Ashes 2013 Second Test at Lord's
Australia 1st Innings 96/7 at tea

The mice had decided to console themselves by watching the cricket. The little group had made their way up through the building and assembled on a ledge above the home dressing room. Tucked just round the corner from the front of the building, the 30-centimetre-wide, lead-covered ledge accommodated them with ease. Even someone with an intimate knowledge of the building would have been hard-pressed to spot them. It was a strangely liberating experience for them to be out in the open in such a public space.

The cricket was gripping. Australian wickets had fallen at regular intervals, and the mice were finding it hard to drag themselves away.

'Okay, one more over,' said Don. 'Then we must get back.'

With the Australian captain starting to look settled on 22, it seemed like a good time to let the game play out a little without their presence. Then a wicket fell.

'We can't go now with a new batsman just in,' pleaded Compo.

'Very well,' Don conceded. 'But at the end of the next over, we should definitely make a move.'

Tantalisingly, the last ball of the next over brought another wicket.

'P-L-E-A-S-E can we stay?' the mice cried in unison.

Don looked to the heavens. What could he say? He wanted to see the next over as much as the others.

Eight overs later, they were still there when a horrible Aussie mix up brought a run out.

'That's it,' Thommo announced. 'I can't watch any more—it's too painful.'

Behind them was a decorative balcony, an architectural feature with no function. It gave access to a ventilation hole for the catering department's lift for carrying food—or 'dumbwaiter'. The party of mice made their way to it to prepare for a swift, if slightly hair-raising, descent.

Downstairs earlier in the afternoon, Basil Ouvry had just finished a game of real tennis on the Lord's court. He was carrying what looked remarkably like a traditional brown leather rectangular shotgun case. What it was in fact was a traditional leather shotgun case that had been cunningly modified to take two real tennis racquets. Keen to catch up on the cricket, he'd popped into the pavilion. However, needing first to visit the gents', he'd nipped down the stairs and rested his case against the wall. In through the 'IN' door of the washroom and out through the 'OUT', he was back up the stairs in no time at all. However, he'd absentmindedly left his case behind.

In no time at all, a public spirited individual had spotted the bag and concerned that it might contain firearms, alerted the assistant in the Members Shop next door to the washroom. So the 'call tree' was activated. Someone called someone else who called someone else, and in no time, Ted the Lord's sniffer dog and his handler had been pressed into action.

Alerted to the situation, a gaggle of stewards arrived well practised in keeping the appearance of calm in a crisis. They firmly but politely steered people away from the area until Ted the Springer spaniel and his 'million-dollar-nose' arrived.

Just above the rectangular leather case, the wooden hatch to the dumbwaiter food lift was framed in the wall. At the top of the shaft, Beefy had overseen the loading of the top of the dumbwaiter's compartment with his friends. Each had had to jump the small gap between the ventilation hole and the top of the box. He'd steadied them as they landed and then settled them, making sure they were well away from any moving parts. Once in position, they'd sat in the relative darkness of the little lift shaft waiting for someone down below to activate it.

Eventually, the lift had shuddered into life after an electrical buzz and started its descent. Down below, Ted was warming to his task, sniffing round the tennis racquet case.

'Normally, if there was anything untoward, he'd have gone ballistic by now,' his handler said. The steward who'd accompanied him and who'd been watching the procedure with interest nodded in agreement.

Above the case, the food lift clunked to a halt. Ted the dog suddenly diverted his attention to the hatch and barked enthusiastically.

'He can smell leftovers,' said the steward.

'No. I don't think so,' Ted's handler replied, his face etched with concern. 'He's really only got a nose for guns and ammunition. Although some people say they can smell guilt. You've not been up to anything, have you?' the handler suddenly challenged the steward.

'What, me?' he stuttered, looking horrified.

'I'm kidding.' The handler clapped the steward on the back. 'I'm satisfied it's nothing to worry about. Let's check and see if there is anything to identify the bag so we can reunite it with its owner.'

All this time, the mice were trapped inside the shaft. They'd climbed down to floor level and were waiting patiently for the coast to clear so they could sneak across the hallway and back into the more easy to navigate internal structure of the building.

Under the Long Room floor, Mrs Heyhoe checked her reflection in a mirror made from a blazer button and straightened her apron. She'd need to be setting out the mouselets' breakfast bowls soon, and there was still a bit of a mess from supper the night before. So much of what went on to ensure the smooth day-to-day running of the colony was down to her. Keeping an eye on the levels of supplies and making lists of what needed to be topped up. Sweeping up the odd dropping from the little ones that might give them away, and just generally keeping the place shipshape.

As she passed the empty cricket net, there was a pile of discarded equipment in a heap—stumps, bats, pads, gloves and helmets. It all took so much effort to create that she hated to see it not looked after. She took a moment to sort it out, leaving the various items in a neat line for some scallywag to come and muddle up again.

The light from Willow's workshop suggested some activity, but there was no sign of anyone. Normally she'd expect to have found at least Don or Beaky. They were always the first up, so to find the place deserted made her a little uncomfortable. At one end of the main thoroughfare was a long since disconnected gas pipe in the shape of an 'f'. It had been inventively turned into a periscope with a fragment of mirror at each end. One end popped up behind the radiator cover grille, it gave her a glimpse of what was happening above ground.

Through the grille she could make out a mass of legs and shoes. The Long Room was chock-a-block, which normally signalled that a session of play was about to end. Mrs Heyhoe relaxed; the boys were bound to be out and about making the most of their access to grandstand seats for an Ashes test. The next break in play would bring them hurrying back, and they'd be hungry. With that in mind, she returned to her preparations for breakfast.

Outside the ground, Skunky and Spotty had pushed, pulled, pleaded, bossed, dragged and partway carried Willow back to the drain in Oak Tree Road. Finally, they'd made it, and Spotty was just poking his nose through the grating to let the others know that they were back when someone called out to him.

'Psst! Over here,' hissed Twitchy, who, living up to his name, was shifting uneasily from foot to foot in the shadows. 'Where have you two been? I've been waiting here in the open for you for ages.'

'Long story,' Spotty said, skipping over to see his friend. Skunky followed him, carrying an exhausted-looking Willow on his back.

'Who's this? Not another mouth to feed when we're already up against it.'

'Hopefully,' Spotty said triumphantly, 'this little lady will sort out our accommodation problem.'

'Oh yeah, well, we've already relocated, but it's just for the time being. That's why I've been waiting here for you. We're all over where the postmen worked. We're in a sort of office.'

What Twitchy meant was the Royal Mail sorting office. It had been empty for some time. The front door was firmly boarded up, and a sign attached to railings warned that it was monitored 24 hours a day by a security company. Not only that, but Pest Arrest had also been employed, and the property was a minefield for any potential unwanted guests.

'I'll take you there now, but...' Twitchy hesitated; there was clearly something he wasn't telling them. 'Just remember that this place is a death trap. We'll stay there just for a short time until we get sorted Bristles says, but we all have to be absolutely on top of our game.'

'It is all right, isn't it?' Skunky asked nervously.

'Yes, it's fine, but as I say, it won't do us long term.'

'And that is because...?' said Spotty.

'As I said, we really have to keep vigilant at all times, as we lost The Dodger today.'

'WE WHAT?' Spotty cried in anguish.

'To a trap,' Twitchy continued. 'There was nothing any of us could do.'

The two rats stared at their friend in disbelief, and Willow shivered.

'Come on, let's go and join the others, best not to dwell on it.'

The empty building was just in the next street, and

they covered the short distance in no time.

'Now try and step where I do; we've done our best to cover up any poison, but the humans who have baited this place with traps are clever and tricky,' Twitchy warned.

Carefully, they descended a set of stone steps, and Twitchy led the way into the building. They flattened themselves against the doorstep and passed through a gap under the door. Inside, Scruffer and Spiff were posted as lookouts.

'Welcome to our new home,' Scruffer announced grandly. 'This way.'

The small group turned a corner and found themselves inside a large rectangular room with a dusty black and white checked floor. There were some pieces of discarded office furniture—desks, chairs, cables, grimy cardboard boxes and some filing cabinets. A wiggly trail worn in the dust that the rats had followed gave away their presence.

Scruffer led the way, and they edged along carefully, warily eyeing the little foil dishes containing deadly pellets that spotted the floor. The path stopped at a great big metal box. An abandoned sorting machine took up most of one wall. The rats had claimed it using the various sections that letters filtered through to house themselves.

'Everyone's in here,' said Scruffer, giving the metal cabinet a bang. Immediately a door at one end opened, and Long Tail looked out.

'We were wondering what had become of you two,' he said abruptly. 'Who's your friend?'

'Where's Bristles? We need to talk to him about her.'

'He's busy right now, Spotty, taking care of The Dodger. You can wait in his den.'

Before long, Bristles returned; he was irritable and distracted.

'You know what happened today?' he challenged Spotty and Skunky. 'Everyone is frightened and upset, and you come and waste my time with this,' he gestured in Willow's direction.

'We know. Who'd have thought The Dodger... he, of all of us,' Spotty paused. 'But because of The Dodger, we need to find somewhere safe to live, and I think this mouse may be able to help us. Look at her, Bristles. She's a beauty—bright eyes, beautiful coat—this is a mouse in the peak of condition.'

'What's your point?' Bristles examined Willow with

his good eye.

'She lives somewhere safe. These mice haven't got the usual problems that city-dwelling rodents have. She could be someone's pet she's in such good health.'

'Yes, I concede she is healthy, but perhaps she *is* someone's pet. We've seen it before.'

'She's not a pet. We saw a man let her go on the other side of the road.'

'You've been to the other side of the road? That was brave if a little foolish.'

'Yes,' Skunky chimed in. 'We got chased by a dog too; we were lucky to get away.'

'What have you got to say for yourself?' Bristles turned his attention to Willow.

Willow turned her face to one side and resolutely ignored him.

Bristles reached over and held her chin between two fingers.

'Tell me something about yourself,' he said calmly.

This sudden change in tone unnerved Willow, but she remained steadfast.

'Tell you? I haven't got anything to tell you. I just want to go home.'

But Willow had inadvertently fallen into a trap.

'So tell me about home, my pretty one.'

'Leave me alone!' Willow pulled her head away.

But Bristles felt the tide turn in his favour, and he pressed on. He leaned over her. Willow felt his hot, rancid breath wash over her. He ran a claw down the side of her face.

'You will tell me where you live... eventually. We can make this as easy or as difficult as you like.'

Spotty looked a bit queasy. He hadn't envisioned such brutal tactics from Bristles.

'Please don't,' Willow cried.

'You will tell me,' Bristles repeated menacingly.

Poor Willow. She realised there would be some confrontation, but she wasn't cut out for this.

'Okay, Skunky,' Bristles said suddenly. 'Take her tail; it looks like it could do with a trim.'

It was too much for her.

'I live in the cricket ground.' The words came in a sudden rush.

'Where exactly?'

'I'll show you if you take me home,' Willow broke down partly due to the ordeal and partly due to the fact that she'd betrayed her friends.

'Give her a break,' Bristles ordered. 'She should rest,

as we've got quite a journey to make later.' And with that, he shooed the little party away.

Willow had protested, but had eventually been settled in a secure part of the sorting machine. Spotty and Skunky stood guard over her. Now left alone, she drifted off into a fitful sleep.

A couple of hours later, she was woken by the sounds of the Pest Arrest operatives arriving to do their rounds of the premises.

'I hate this bloomin' thing,' said one as he attempted to negotiate a tight doorway with an awkward wheeled cabinet. He lost his temper with it and tried to force it through the space, trapping his fingers against the doorframe.

'Yeeeouch!' he yelled, pulling off his glove and throwing it to the ground in a child-like tantrum.

'Stanley, we've got a long night ahead of us, and there's no point getting all worked up over such a little thing,' Bob, his older, wiser colleague suggested. 'Look, if I get on one end, and we give it a bit of a jiggle... there, see? That wasn't so bad after all.'

Stanley blew on his sore fingers and nodded his agreement.

'We've got to check and re-bait all the traps here,

replenish the feed stations and check for any new points of entry. Then we're off to Lord's Cricket Ground. That'll be fun, won't it?'

The rats had been alerted to the men's presence by the metallic banging of the cabinet. The older males watched the men intently from various vantage points within the sorting machine. Having wheeled it to the centre of the room, Stanley unhitched the cabinet door and got to work.

'Did you hear that, Bristles? They're going to the Cricket Ground,' one of Bristles' lieutenants urged him.

'I did indeed, Spiff, and I think I know how we're going to get there,' he nodded in the direction of the cabinet. 'Go and get our lady friend.'

Bob and Stanley went about their business collecting various concoctions from the cabinet and transferring them to different locations. One trap seemed to be of particular interest.

'Look, Bob, this has been sprung, but there's no body.'

While the men examined The Dodger's last port of call, Bristles, Spiff, Twitchy and Spotty swiftly left the safety of their hiding place and sped over to the cabinet. Twitchy had a bulging bag slung across his back that contained their mousey bargaining chip.

Onto the bottom shelf of the metal box they jumped, slinking in amongst its contents. The rats squeezed themselves into the darkest recesses of the cabinet and waited. Each of them nervously eyed the potentially deadly bottles and substances they were pressed up against. Bob and Stanley returned and fussed about their supplies.

'There, a good job jobbed,' Bob announced, closing the cabinet door with a clang. 'Let's get your favourite thing back into the van and head over to Lord's.'

Once out in the street, they manhandled their cabinet and its opportunistic cargo into their vehicle and drove the short distance to the Grace Gates. In an unlikely twist, the two Pest Arrest employees inadvertently delivered another group of pests to the home of cricket.

Chapter Seven

Close of play on the second day
England 2nd Innings 31 for 3 – a lead of 264

McCrackers marched down to the Grace Gates with a spring in his step. Despite a clatter of wickets at the end of the day, England were in a strong position. However, when playing Australia, one never wanted to be complacent.

'We've had a good day, Sir Sidney,' McCrackers quipped to Sid Pickett as he pushed his way out through the portable turnstiles.

'Aye, not bad, but I've been an England fan too long to count my chickens,' Sid replied mournfully. 'You're off early for you.'

'Yes, I've been invited to a charity do,' McCrackers announced, rubbing his tummy. 'While you, I'm afraid, look as though you're in for a busy evening.' McCrackers nodded in the direction of the white van that was trying to pull in through the gates.

Sid looked at his clipboard, registered a tick on the document attached to it and stepped out of his gatekeeper's cabin.

Stanley wound down the window on the passenger's side.

'Are we in the right place, mate?' he asked loudly.

'Yes,' Sid replied, irritably handing over two pass badges. 'If you could remember to make your visit as low-key as possible, I'd be much obliged. If you drive straight in past the pavilion under the arch and park up just beyond it.'

'We're not going to have to carry our gear far, are we?' Stanley moaned.

'That'll be fine,' Bob leaned across him to interrupt, remembering the old saying about the customer always being right.

'Once you've parked, if you could wait in your vehicle, I'll see to it that someone comes to escort you,' Sid instructed.

Having driven in, they'd been stationary for a few minutes when Mr Hobbs appeared.

'I'm so sorry to keep you, gentlemen; it has turned out to be a busy evening. At the moment, I've got the TV people in the Long Room adjusting their cameras. It's the first time they've been allowed to film inside the pavilion, and as this is an Ashes test match, it's a bit of a big deal.'

The Pest Arrest crew murmured their understanding, even though one of them didn't actually understand at all.

'Sorry,' said Stanley, 'you've lost me. What is an 'Ashes'?'

Mr Hobbs looked amazed.

'You don't know about *The* Ashes.'

'Nope, I guess I don't.'

Mr Hobbs looked at his watch. 'Tell you what. They're going to be another twenty minutes. I'll show you something interesting. Follow me.'

Mr Hobbs led the two men across the way and unlocked a glazed door.

'Just a moment,' he advised, ducking inside to disarm the alarm.

'Right, follow me.'

Mr Hobbs led the way into the Lord's Museum. A large, airy space consisting of two floors decked out with glass cabinets full of cricketing memorabilia.

'We'll find what we're looking for on the next floor up.' Mr Hobbs pointed ahead, ushering the two men up a quite grand set of stone stairs.

For the series against Australia, the curator of the museum had organised a special 'Ashes' exhibition, and in the middle of it was a square glass cabinet housing the 11-centimetre-high terracotta Ashes Urn.

'There you are,' Mr Hobbs announced triumphantly. 'The Ashes.'

'You are kidding me,' said Stanley.

'Absolutely not. That is what they are playing for, the most prized object in the cricketing world.'

Mr Hobbs went on to explain that the Australian's first victory on English soil was reported as the death of English cricket. As a result, the body, it was said, should be cremated and the ashes, in the urn, taken to Australia.

Stanley was still shaking his head as Mr Hobbs locked up the museum again. Just at that moment, two technicians carrying aluminium-covered suitcases came out of the pavilion opposite.

'Ahh, look, here come the TV people now—perfect timing. Thank you for your patience. Perhaps you can start unloading your equipment.'

The men agreed and started to unload the van while Mr Hobbs nipped into the pavilion to prop the doors open for them. He was surprised to see through the Long Room windows that on the playing surface there was a cluster of bright lights. He went to investigate and was met at the central double door by a pretty blonde girl.

'Hi, I'm Natasha, the TV director's assistant. We're just having a run through of the awards ceremony.'

Mr Hobbs looked over at the small stage and the ex-England captain, now commentator, being put through his paces.

'Poor dear, he absolutely hates this bit. It's a pity really because he's really quite good, but he gets terrible stage fright.'

To one side of the stage, a small boy was bowling to a make-believe batsman against the pavilion fence.

'He's got some stamina,' Mr Hobbs acknowledged.

'Yes, he's been here with his dad all day. Quite mind blowing for a little boy to see behind the scenes, but he's been as good as gold. No trouble at all.'

Mr Hobbs took his leave of the girl and disappeared. He returned almost instantly pushing a wheeled curtain. He pushed it to one end of the room and set it up in front of the radiator cover. When he was satisfied that the Pest Arrest men would be suitably concealed, he went off to find them.

The metal cabinet was once again proving to have a mind of its own, and its wheels rolled in every direction but the right one. Stanley cursed it and the metal door opened and banged about.

'Please be careful of the paintwork,' Mr Hobbs pleaded.

'Oi, Stan, go and get some of that spongy stuff from the van to protect the doorway.'

'But I've got to get the electro snake thingy... and the bait. I haven't got three pairs of arms.'

'All right, all right, calm down. I'll come too.'

'Can I be of assistance?' Mr Hobbs asked.

'Well, it would speed things up,' Bob admitted.

So the three left the Long Room to fetch the items from the van. It gave the rats the ideal opportunity to escape. The cabinet door was already ajar, and as they listened to the retreating footsteps, the rats edged out of their hiding place. Twitchy lowered his bag to the floor and its contents writhed about.

For a moment, the four rats stood stunned at the grand setting they found themselves in. The Long Room stretched away from them as far as the eye could see it seemed. The walls hung with imposing pictures of past cricketers, and everything lit by three striking chandeliers.

'Where are we?' Spiff wondered dreamily.

'This is what I imagine a palace must look like,' Spotty added.

'Hopefully it will be our new home,' Bristles cut in. 'But we better look lively about it, or the humans will be back. Twitchy, the bag, please.'

Twitchy untied the top of the bag and shook its contents to the floor. Willow was disorientated and blinded momentarily, having been kept in the dark. She sensed freedom, however, and ran skittishly this way and that before bumping into a wall. Spotty picked her up and slipped a makeshift string leash over her head. Bristles arrived at his shoulder.

'Now show us where to go,' he said.

Willow looked up at him and weighed up her chances of giving the rats the slip.

'You're not having second thoughts now, are you? If we don't get on with it, the humans will be back, and then we'll all be sorry.'

Willow nodded her agreement and set off. With Twitchy running in her wake and the others in pursuit, they ran the length of the Long Room. They hugged the skirting for cover and then at the last moment darted across the room and under the radiator cover. Moments later, the three men returned to find the room just as they'd left it.

Behind the radiator cover, the rodents had slipped down through the skirting. Willow was eager to be reunited with her friends, and she strained against her leash. Twitchy had banged his head quite hard on the way through, but that was the least of his problems. What the rats hadn't counted on were the dimensions of the mouse world below the floor. At twice the size of the mice, it was a tight fit. Willow threaded her way down through the floorboards while the rats bumped and bashed their way down. It was as though the mouse had deliberately set an assault course of sharp edges to snag on and overhead obstructions to dodge.

Willow arrived in the open space to find the cricket net in use. Thommo was bowling some of his slingy fast deliveries at Compo, who was resolutely defending.

Thommo spotted Willow first.

'Oi, mate!' he cried. 'Would ya look at who just walked in.'

Compo looked behind him and then dropped his bat in disbelief.

'WILLOW!' he cried, running into the net and getting tangled up in it. He threw off his various pieces of cricket protection as he tried to disentangle himself.

Eventually, he was able to run round and hug his friend.

'My goodness, you're squashing me,' Willow squeaked.

Thommo, meanwhile, was stirring up further excitement, spreading the news to anyone who could hear him.

'WILLOW'S BACK, EVERYBODY, SHE'S ALIVE!' he called.

"Oh, Willow, it's so good to see you,' Compo beamed as he continued to hug his friend. Then he noticed her string leash.

'What's this?'

Some of the others were just starting to appear. Heads poked out of dormitories, and some of the mice came down the corridor excited by the news that was being passed through the colony. But as they arrived, the bad news that had accompanied Willow finally made it into the space.

'I'm so sorry, everybody, they made me do it,' Willow sobbed, slumping to the floor.'

Twitchy appeared snout first, and there was a collective gasp from the mice that had responded to Thommo's call.

The other rats crowded their way into the space,

filling it. Compo cowered slightly in their presence but bravely stood his ground, shielding Willow. Natural selection took over with the younger mice backing away and the senior figures of the colony inching forward.

Bristles pushed past the other rats and menacingly looked about him.

'This is very cosy, I must say.'

Don and Beefy had made their way to the front of the group to confront them with some of the braver mice—Gatt, WG, and Fred shadowing them.

'Welcome,' Don ventured.

Beefy did a double take at Don's greeting and added his own welcome.

'Clear off! This is no place for your sort.'

Bristles leaned in to Beefy.

'Oh okay, excuse us,' he said with a leer before swatting Beefy to one side.

'Steady on,' Don broke in. 'We don't want any of your roughhousing in our home.'

'You seem to be under the misapprehension that you're in charge here.'

'Yeah, we're in charge,' Spotty added.

Bristles looked testily over his shoulder at this

unwanted contribution.

'And I'm interested to hear you say your home. Because I'm just starting to feel quite at home here myself.'

'You certainly look pretty snug,' Beefy observed, picking himself up.

Gatt smirked at the dig, which resulted in a withering look from Bristles.

'We could be pretty comfortable here,' Bristles said, looking about him.

'Clearly you would be if it was an option, which it isn't,' Don added hastily. 'Such an idea isn't practical... on so many levels.'

'Well, as I see it,' Bristles continued, 'my friends and I and our little ones are looking for a new home, and this would be just perfect. All we need for that to happen is for you to pack your little bags and get outta here.' He jabbed a thumb over his shoulder.

Beefy joined Don and linked his arm through his friends.

'That isn't going to happen.'

Gatt joined them, followed by WG and Fred.

'Touching, very touching, don't you think, boys?'

'Yeah, very swee-t.' Twitchy spat the 't'. 'It's all very

sad and that, but you little guys are history, and we're moving in.'

Don swallowed hard and took a step forward.

'No, no, you don't understand. This place is special, and our link with it is one of generations on generations,' he explained earnestly. 'There have been mice here since 1890, almost since the last spot of paint dried. Heritage and history and love for a game that this place embodies are all tied up here.'

'Game?' Bristles enquired.

'Cricket, this is the home of cricket.'

'Cricket, I hate cricket,' Spiff said ungraciously. 'Football, now that's a rat's game.'

'Precisely my point,' Don reasoned.

Bristles blew out his cheeks in exasperation.

'Anyway, whatever, this has all been very pleasant, but I think it's time to get you lot out,' Bristles ordered.

'No, wait, you have to give us a chance,' Beefy said, his tone more measured than before. 'We'll play for it, fair and square. A game of cricket to decide who gets to stay. If we lose, we'll go.'

Bristles looked the mouse up and down. He was starting to show his age. His close-cropped fur showed tinges of grey, but there was something about him. An indefinable strength that was unnerving.

'Smash him, Bristles,' Spotty advised.

Bristles held up his hand. He might be a bit rough and ready, but he admired the mouse's sense of honour. It was a quality that he prided himself on and what he owed his ability to keep the rats' community together.

'All right, a game of cricket will decide it.'

'Naaaa,' cried Spiff. 'Just bash him.'

Bristles flashed an angry look at him. 'It's fair, and I've decided.'

In the Long Room, Mr Hobbs had left the men to their own devices. Stanley was unwinding the 'electro snake thingy.' It was actually an inspection camera on a fibreglass cable ideal for inspecting an underground narrow space. Bob had carefully removed the radiator cover, and the entrance to the mouse residence was all too apparent.

'Here we are,' Bob said triumphantly. 'There's plenty of activity here—clever little blighters. Stanley, the mouse scope if you please.'

Stanley dutifully handed the camera end of the cable to Bob. Having made sure the light on the end was functioning, he fed the cable down through the floorboards.

Below the floor, Spiff was the first to become aware of the intrusive camera as it poked him sharply in the rear.

'Oi, what the...?'

But some of the older mice had seen this before.

'Quick! Into the dormitories! Press yourselves to the very back, and don't move a muscle,' Don cried.

He didn't need to give the order twice. The mice had a very strong sense of self-preservation and often followed such drills. The rats, however, were thrown into confusion. One moment the mice had been there, the next they'd disappeared. The rats dived for what cover they could find, but not before Bob had seen something he hadn't been expecting on his monitor.

'Stanley, take a look. I hadn't expected this.'

But by the time Stanley looked, the rats had managed to make themselves scarce.

Below, the floor the camera swept about like a snake with a headlamp. The rodents kept well out of its way, which was proving frustrating for those up above.

'I tell you I saw a rat down there.'

'No, mate, you must be losing it. That hole is far too small for a rat.'

'I'm telling you what I saw and they...' he gestured

with a nod of his head towards an imaginary MCC member, '... are not going to like it.'

'Don't go setting off alarm bells without proof though, mate.'

'You're right.' Bob looked around uneasily. 'We'll bait here for both 'eventualities' if you know what I mean and hope that sorts things out.'

The camera was pulled out, and the mice and rats came out from their hiding places.

Bristles and Don came head to head again.

'So this cricket match, when's it going to be?'

'You'll need to practice I'm guessing.' Don looked towards the footballing Spiff. 'So shall we say the night after next. We can supply you with bats and pads, but they might be a bit small.'

'Don't you worry about us. We'll see what we can come up with. So, where's it going to be, this winner-takes-all game?'

'Well, since the stakes are so high, I think upstairs would be fitting, in the Long Room.'

'Yeah, I like the idea of that, very lah-de-dah,' he smirked in a mock posh accent. 'How are we going to get back in though?'

'That's no problem; I'll get someone to show you.'

With that, Bristles and Don shook hands. Beefy mooched over and gruffly shook hands too.

'Gatt, can you show these err... gentlemen out through the 'thunderbox'?''

'Leaving so soon?' he said sarcastically. It would be my pleasure to throw them... I mean *show* them out.'

So the rats left the mice to contemplate the events that had just taken place in their home. Gatt led the way to a path to one side of their usual entrance.

'Why's it called the 'thunderbox'?' Spotty asked.

'I'll show you.'

The mouse ran along a path that followed the line of the floor joist. Viewed from above, their path had taken them from the Long Room, across the corridor and now they were beneath the Committee Room.

'Here,' said Gatt. 'We turn here and go down this tube.'

On the joist above the tube in cursive Victorian handwriting was the word 'Thunderbox'.

'What does it mean?' asked Twitchy.

'I have no idea,' said Gatt as he disappeared down it.

What it was in fact was the plumbing for a Victorian portable toilet for the delicate members of the committee to relieve themselves in. The 'thunderbox' had been in an early design for the pavilion, but had been ruled out as being unsanitary. The plumbing had been put in place and then the plan had changed. So the mice were provided with the perfect way in and out of the pavilion if they needed it.

Gatt was looking forward to getting rid of the unwanted guests and ran ahead. It was downhill all the way, and soon he was at the exit. The drain came out at one end of the banked seating in front of the pavilion, one of a series of four holes in the brickwork. At the exit, Gatt gave the rats instructions.

'From here, your best way is to cut straight across the ground. They'll be no one around now.'

'Now we know the way in, you know we can come and visit any time, and next time it'll be for good,' Bristles warned.

The other rats sniggered as they ran past Gatt, who couldn't resist kicking the last one as firmly in the rump as he could.

It was a cheap shot, and immediately Gatt regretted it. Twitchy span round and in one movement pinned him to the floor of the drain.

'Right, you asked for it,' he threatened, grasping Gatt by the throat.

At that moment, the boy who was still patiently playing on the outfield bowled his ball through the railings. Because of the slope on the ground, the railings were too high to reach over. His dad spotted him struggling and called out.

'There are steps at the far end.'

The boy followed the instruction and ran round to the end of the bank of seating. His arrival coincided with the imminent demise of Gatt.

The sudden sound of the boy's arrival distracted Twitchy, and Gatt was able to wriggle out of his clutches. It was a close escape, and as he ran back up the pipe, Twitchy called after him, his voice echoing.

'We'll be back!'

Chapter Eight

Day Three of the Ashes second test

The mice had taken comfort in their togetherness. Holed up in the 'bothy', they'd talked long into the night about the evening's events. Although the rats had long gone, their home felt as if it had been violated.

The ladies were concerned.

'I cannot believe you bet our home on a cricket match,' Mrs Beefy scolded.

'It isn't as though we had a choice; it was more of an ultimatum.'

'Actually, given the odds, I think the boys did quite well to buy us some time,' Mrs Beaky reasoned.

'They were all for walking us out there and then. That would have been devastating for us all, especially the little ones,' WG explained while winding his wispy beard with his fingers.

'But is it not just a matter of time?' Mrs Ranji asked, looking worried.

'Don't worry, dear,' Ranji said, doing his best to soothe her by putting his arm round her.

'It will take a concerted effort from us all,' said Don.

'We boys need to whip ourselves into shape. The team pretty much picks itself, but there's plenty to do if we're going to stage this match.'

'I'm keen that you look the part,' Mrs Heyhoe added. 'So you can count on me for a little surprise for you all. Perhaps some of the other ladies can help with some of the other chores. We'll need a physio and first-aider.'

'What about the catering?' asked Gatt. 'It's very important. I love my cricket tea.'

'Hey you, you're on a diet,' Mrs Gatt warned. 'Anyway, you boys are just as capable as us of rustling up a couple of snacks.'

'One thing that doesn't need slimming down is my bat. Thank goodness Willow's back,' Beefy beamed. 'I'm going to need the biggest, finest one she's ever created.'

Everyone voiced his or her agreement.

Don was pretty happy with the feel-good factor that had been generated. There were still some members that needed to be drawn in, and he knew just how to do so.

'CMJ, you'll oversee the scoring and make sure the laws of cricket are adhered to.'

'What? Err... oh... well... I see...'

'I'll think that means that you will. Meanwhile,

Bumble, if you and Compo can take care of the wicket, boundary markers and a scoreboard, that would be grand. Can you see to that?'

'Righto,' Bumble agreed with a salute, and Compo nodded.

So plans were made into the small hours of the morning before the mouse community turned in for perhaps their last but one sleep in the pavilion.

The morning of the third day of the test was cloudy, but the sun was expected to burn through. McCrackers arrived at the ground by taxi and was just paying his fare. Normally, he wouldn't have been so extravagant, but today he had on his full regalia. Red trousers, club tie, yellow shirt, red and yellow stripy blazer and straw boater complete with red and yellow hatband. The Headingly test match tradition of 'fancy dress' Saturday had had a knock-on effect throughout the country. Lord's was never going to get to grips with the idea fully. If, however, anyone had a jacket that needed a volume control in their wardrobe, today was the day they'd wear it.

'Very smart, Mr McTavish,' Sid Pickett observed at the gate.

'What these old things? Do you really think so?' McCrackers said casually, loving the attention.

A girl in a red outfit offered him a 4 and 6 card emblazoned with a sponsor's name. Normally McCrackers would have dismissed her, but he was in a surprisingly good mood, and the girl was particularly pretty.

'Well, my dear, that's very kind of you, but...'

At that moment, a scrawny-looking cat slunk across his path. The cat had come from the direction of the Harris Garden. The rose garden situated just before the pavilion was another popular spot for diners and a hot spot for would-be scavengers.

'The place is turning into a zoo,' McCrackers spluttered, making a shooing noise at the cat. Despite the casualness the cat had shown up to now, McCrackers' outburst made him lengthen his stride and he skipped away.

'Look at that cheeky fellow, bold as brass,' McCrackers called after him. The cat looked back at him and in that instant a waiter carrying a pile of metal trays tripped over him. The resulting clatter made the cat bolt, and in doing so, he dropped what was in his mouth.

A small form fell to the ground, the fall and landing knocking the last bit of wind out of it.

An 'Oouff!' accompanied the final sound of its deflating. On the tarmac lay the limp form of a long, thin and gangly mouse. He lay still for an instant, believing that somehow he'd successfully made the passage to mouse heaven. The scraping sound of the trays being gathered brought him to his senses. He sat up and patted himself down. Despite its sharp teeth, the cat had failed to puncture him at all. He'd endured a bit of an ordeal as it had patted him about a bit, and he was certainly a bit scratched. When the cat had taken him up in his mouth, he'd fallen into a sort of unconscious state—zoning out the inevitable. But here he was, very much alive. He perked up considerably at the thought and looked about him for a means of escape.

He was between two buildings, the pavilion and the Allen Stand. Ahead of him there was an endless carpet of green. That was no use to him, as he needed cover. To his left there was a wall with four equally spaced holes at the bottom of it. The first one was blocked, the second was not, that was all he needed, and without hesitation he disappeared up it.

Inside the pavilion, preparations were well in hand for the start of the day's play. The bell on the small balcony outside the Bowler's Bar was about to be rung. Today's ringer was an Australian player who in the seventies was considered a hard and fiery competitor. Now in his sixties, he didn't appear frightening at all. In fact, the talk today was more about Australia requiring a miracle to save the game than them trouncing their old rivals.

In the changing rooms, the two teams had gone through their last-minute match day routines. In the Australian dressing room, the wicketkeeper went through the ritual of binding up his fingers. The endless thud of the ball into his gloves had taken its toll. It seemed that the amount of protective tape he applied went up with each match. One thumb, two forefingers, a middle finger on one hand, a wrist and most painful of all, the middle joint of a little finger. He'd run his inner gloves under the tap before putting them on, then finally the all-important blue and white gauntlets. Some players talked of superstitions. One Australian captain always liked the same seat in the Lord's away dressing room. But there was no room for such distractions today.

In the England dressing, the two 'not out' batsmen had their own routines. Maybe they'd put on one particular pad first, but neither of them would admit to being superstitious. Red rags, blue socks, green socks and threadbare caps all these items had been used to ward off jinxes by past international players. A newspaper journalist had written that one player padding up was half of the thirteenth father and son combination to play for England.

'Good job I'm not superstitious,' he'd replied calmly when shown it.

So with nothing more than their hundreds of pounds worth of kit, the gift of talent and the hopes of a nation, the two batters walked out through the dressing room door.

The walk to the wicket at Lord's is pretty straightforward as long as you remember how many flights of stairs you have to take. Famously, the Northamptonshire cricketer David Steele on his test match debut got lost and ended up in the basement. So after the *two* flights of stairs, you enter the Long Room and receive a warm welcome from the members gathered there. One Australian batsman had described the sensation as 'being bear-hugged by an invisible spirit'. Through the Long Room and then out through the doors to the middle. This is the point that the rest of the crowd gets their first glimpse of the players and the applause builds to its peak.

Meanwhile, outside the ground, while the professionals got down to business, a more amateur outfit was being put through its paces. Stinger had found a scrunched-up copy of a match programme. It was a useful starting point. The rats had poured over it, analysing batting and bowling techniques from the pictures.

Bristles had identified the core members of his team. There were those who were fittest or showed natural agility. He had a couple of other spots to fill and had taken a gamble with Rags and Fleabag, who was not a natural athlete. Mr Cheese was also on standby to be abrasive and awkward should the need arise.

The little group had assembled in the stairwell outside their temporary home. It provided an ideal practice area, as it was enclosed and free of any potentially lethal rat-hunting devices. Bristles had put Stinger in charge of the training, as he was generally acknowledged as being the most sporty and also knew a bit about cricket.

He'd taken to his task with relish, insisting that before they did anything, they needed to assemble some kit. The professionals nearby had unpacked a seemingly endless supply of plastic-bagged, pristine, brand-new gear whereas the rats had improvised. Fortunately for them, the local council had tried to brighten up a featureless concrete structure by planting colourful climbing plants. To do this, they'd fixed a wooden trellis of interwoven pieces of wood. These slats, if removed by, say, an industrious furry type with sharp teeth, were the ideal width for 'ratty' bats. Balls had come courtesy of the colony's supply of hazel nuts buried under a nearby telephone box.

So the training session had begun.

'You big guys are going to have a bowl.' Stinger armed his stable of would be bowlers with hazelnut balls. 'And you, my great batting hopefuls, are going to have a bat.'

Stinger had scratched a rudimentary set of stumps on the brick wall at one end of the stairwell. Someone had found a roll of bubble wrap, and each of the batmen had fixed a length of it to their shins as pads. Stinger handed one of the team bats to Twitchy and set him up in front of the stumps.

'Now, Spiff, bowl a ball and let's see how we get on.'

Spiff stepped up, weighed the hazelnut in his hand and sized up the distance between them. He closed one eye, jammed his tongue into the corner of his mouth and threw the nut as hard as he could. Twitchy was living up to his name and jumping skittishly from one leg to the other. He saw the nut for an instant and then firmly closed both his eyes. He whirled the bat about him like a helicopter blade and spanked the nut back over Spiff's head.

'Goal!' Twitchy cried.

Stinger put his head in his hands.

'I see we've got some way to go.'

'I don't think it was a bad start at all. Let me have a go,' Bristles said importantly, pushing Twitchy to one side.

'Spiff, you just chucked the ball; you need to *bowl* it.' Stinger mimed a quite decent bowling action, rolling his arm over.

Spiff acted it out.

'That's it,' Stinger complimented him.

Spiff stepped up and this time bowled the ball. Bristles firmly gripped the bat and waited. The ball was released and flew towards Bristles. He didn't move a muscle and the ball spiralled in and struck him on the chest.

'Oi, don't just throw it at me, wait until I'm ready.'

But Bristles had been ready, he'd just not seen the ball out of his blind left eye.

'I'm really sorry, mate,' Spiff apologised, 'but you looked straight at me.'

Now Bristles was embarrassed, and his embarrassment turned to anger.

Stinger stepped in.

'Wait a minute, I think I know what the problem is,' he grabbed Bristles and turned him round to a left-handed batting stance.

'Give it another go.'

Spiff bowled the ball. Bristles watched the flight of it. The ball pitched, and he stretched out a foot to meet it. The bat came down in a smooth arc and cleanly drove the ball back past the bowler.

'Shot of the day!' Stinger congratulated him.

The other bowlers now stepped up to have a go. A succession of full tosses, donkey drops, wides and pea-rollers followed. Stinger despaired.

'You're all trying to bowl too fast; take it easy. Rooooll your arm over like this. Try and look where you're bowling. Imagine putting the ball on a particular spot,' he directed.

Bitesize, then Long Tail, then Spotty, then Skunky tried with varying degrees of success. Rags, who had been standing around watching and had been overlooked for either group, thought he'd try his hand. He picked up one of the nuts and rolled his arm over slowly, the nut ripping out of the back of his hand. The ball pitched and spun to the left sharply.

'Hey, you can't do that!' cried Fleabag, who was having a bat and not finding it easy.

Stinger, who was concentrating on the set up of Scruffer's batting stance, looked up.

'Can't do what?'

'He bowled a spinner! That's not fair, is it?'

'Do it again, Rags,' Stinger instructed.

Rags bowled again, and the ball turned away from the batsman's bat.

'A leg break! You've just bowled a leg break.'

'I don't want my leg broken,' Fleabag whimpered.

Spiff was pretty happy with the way the training was going. He had four decent batsmen and a couple of bowlers he could rely on. He'd be able to bat a bit and bowl if needed.

'Right, everyone gather round.'

The rats did as they were told.

'Now that we've got the basics of batting and bowling, we need to look at our fielding. Remember, catches win matches.'

Stinger had a stick with a blob of chewing gum on the end, which he stuck on the ground.

'Everybody spread out around me.' He gestured to the farthest points of the stairwell. 'I'm going to randomly hit the ball to you. It might come at you along the ground or it might be a catch. The main thing is that whatever happens, the ball doesn't get past you, right? Then when you have the ball, I want you to throw the ball into the wicketkeeper standing by the stump.' Stinger stopped. He had no wicketkeeper.

The wicketkeeper is an important position. It requires a combination of athleticism, coordination, confidence and an 'x' factor which in the nicest possible terms is to be a little bit bonkers.

'Spotty, come and have a go at being wicketkeeper.'

He scampered over and having had bubble wrap wrapped around his hands for gloves, Spotty took up his position.

'Here goes.' Stinger hoisted a catch in the direction

of Long Tail with a bat.

After a moment's hesitation, Long Tail reacted to the call and watched the ball travel through the air towards him. He stretched up his hands to catch it. Suddenly realising that he'd misjudged the catch, he ran towards it, tripping over his tail as he did so. However, all the time he kept his eye on the ball and his hands outstretched. In the end, what had been a clumsy fall turned into a spectacular catch.

'Great catch!' Stinger complimented, giving him a clap. 'Now get it in to Spotty.'

The throw came in a little wayward, but Spotty was able to catch it. 'Well done, everybody. Let's have a few more of those.'

It seemed that the game of cricket had some unlikely converts. Once they'd started, no one wanted to stop. The bowlers wanted a bat and the batters a bowl.

'I'll tell you what we'll do, we'll pair off with a partner and then take it in turns batting together while the others bowl and field. How does that sound?' Stinger suggested.

Everyone thought this was a great idea. It also introduced an aspect of the game that up until now had been overlooked—how the batsmen might be dismissed. This new feature was to provide an element of disagreement between the participants that gave Stinger something else to manage.

Back inside Lord's, things were progressing a little more sedately. England had managed to add just 83 runs before a break, extending their lead. The crowd gratefully adjourned for lunch. When the cricketers returned, there were more empty seats than usual at the front of the pavilion as friends extended their get-togethers. Joe Root brought them back to their seats as he edged towards a century, and then as the excitement built, the clock ticked round to teatime. Root, not out on 97, got a resounding cheer as he walked back to the pavilion. Beneath the terraced seating, the escapologist mouse who had been taking a rather unfortunately named catnap woke up.

Sleep had stiffened him up after his ordeal at the paws of his assailant. He stretched and started to make his way up the slope ahead of him. It seemed quite a steep and difficult climb. He was already weak given all he'd been put through, and this was really going to take it out of him.

At the other end of the 'thunderbox', Compo was customising a triangular desk calendar. It was a bit dusty and creased, but with some minor adjustments it would make a perfect scoreboard. He'd labelled it at the top with 'Mouse Cricket Club' and 'The Rat Packers'. He'd drawn a not very flattering rat under the name. They could cross off the days of each month as runs were scored, and he drew a column on each side to keep a tally of wickets lost. He'd just stepped back to admire his handiwork when the lanky mouse appeared at the top of the pipe.

'Might I trouble you for a drink of water?' he asked and fainted.

Chapter Nine

Day Three of the Ashes second test
Close of play England 333-5

It had taken Joe Root a nerve-jangling three overs to add to his teatime score of 97 not out. Then at the beginning of the fourth over after tea came a two and then a 4 and everyone wondered what they'd been worrying about. He'd become the youngest England player to score a century in a test match at Lord's. Someone had written his details on a piece of tape in black marker pen. This had been stuck on the honours board in the home changing room until a sign-writer could make it official. With his contribution, England had finished the day with an overall lead of 566 over Australia.

This sort of position of dominance is not an everyday occurrence for the England cricket team. Despite this fact, there was one person in the ground who was not pleased with the way the day had ended. 566 runs in the lead, but 333, triple Nelson, on the board. It seems unlikely that Admiral Horatio Nelson should be to blame. One eye, one arm, one leg, despite the fact that Nelson never lost a leg, the score in cricket of 111 is known as 'Nelson'. One eye, one arm and one lump of sugar others claimed. Whatever the origin, multiply that by three, then if you're the superstitious sort, like McCrackers, you're in trouble. Bad things happen on 'Nelson' unless you keep one leg in the air. This, it is believed, will ward off evil hexes. Which is fine if you've just got to wait for a couple of balls for the score to change, but overnight?

The secretary had had a relatively carefree day. On the first day of the test, he'd had the visit of Her Majesty the Queen to worry about. On Friday the Prime Minister had dropped in. Today he'd been able to pop in and out of the Committee Room and enjoy the cricket. He'd rubbed shoulders with the great and the good of the cricketing world—one of the perks that went with his post. The weather forecast was good. The odds stacked in England's favour, and nothing could dampen his mood as he meandered from one room to another. He hadn't counted on finding McCrackers in distress.

'Aha, am I glad to see you, dear boy.'

He was leaning against one of the long tables set in the middle of the Long Room having hopped there.

'Any chance you could get someone to find me a wheelchair?'

'Erm, I don't believe that's actually a service we provide.'

'Come on, you must have one tucked away for just this sort of thing. You know, the score, we're on triple Nelson. Someone has to take responsibility for the team's good fortune.'

'I'm sure the combined England team and backroom staff would be alarmed to think that their fate rests in your hands. Or rather feet.' The secretary stifled a snigger.

'You might laugh, remember Headingly in 1981?'

For a moment, the secretary reflected on the momentous events that saw England turn defeat into miraculous victory over Australia. Surely the boot couldn't be on the other foot—McCrackers' foot at that.

The secretary was saved by the arrival of a presenter from the TV company. He pushed a microphone under McCrackers' nose while the cameraman shadowing him filmed the event.

'Would you like to comment on there being TV cameras in the pavilion for the first time?'

'What, me on the television? Do you think that's a

good idea? Are we live?' asked McCrackers, adjusting his tie.

'Good Luck,' the secretary said to the presenter, grabbing the opportunity to escape.

The cameraman framed the shot, and McCrackers selected his best side for the interview. For a few moments, the more eccentric side of the cricket-watching public got its few minutes of fame.

At that moment, any sharp-eyed viewers would have noticed a mouse wearing a chef's hat in the bottom right-hand corner of the screen. Bumble had helped himself to the contents of a box marked 'Cutlet Frills' that he'd found in a storage cupboard. These little paper chefs' hats were used to dress pork chops and other cuts of meat. He'd found them whilst looking for boundary markers, and to Bumble, they looked very useful indeed. He'd stacked six together, which he stuffed under one arm, and another four that he was wearing on his head. If several hundred people did shout at their television screen 'Look, there's a mouse!' no one in the Long Room reacted. Before anyone was any the wiser, he'd darted out of sight beneath the radiator cover to safety.

Bumble pushed his useful find through the

entrance hole and followed it down into the mouse residence. A small gathering had formed at the junction where the entrances to the upstairs world and 'thunderbox' met.

'Anyone like a hat?' Bumble asked brightly.

'Oooh, Bumble, you and your larking around; your timing is terrible,' Compo scolded him.

Bumble was a little taken aback to be lectured then noticed that the little group were tending to someone lying on the ground.

'Oh no, they haven't been poisoned, have they?'

When he'd left that morning, a small team wearing aprons made from yellow rubber gloves had been dispatched to clear away the poisoned bait left by Pest Arrest.

'No, I don't think he'd still be with us if that were the case. Give us a hand and we'll get him down to Mrs Heyhoe.'

There was plenty of excitement at the new arrival below the Long Room. Mrs Heyhoe had revived him with some of her soaked sultana juice, and Beefy led the questioning.

'So, what's your name, son?'

'Mikey, sir,' he responded respectfully.

'You don't need to call me 'sir',' he said kindly. 'That's quite an accent you have, where are you from?'

'My family live in Notting Hill, but my great, great grandfather travelled to England on a cruise ship from Jamaica.'

'So, if you've got Jamaican ancestors, do you like cricket?'

'I don't *like* cricket, I LURVE IT!' Mikey suddenly cheered up.

'Well, you've ended up in the right place then. How come you're so far from home?'

'My family and I live next to a bakery, and I was inspecting, if you know what I mean, their donuts... when the tray I was in got loaded onto a truck. Next thing I know, I'm a million miles from home being batted about by some dirty great big cat with sharp claws.'

'Hmm, Tufnell the cat. You were unlucky to be caught by him.'

'Today hasn't exactly been a lucky day. Fortunately, he dropped me and I got away. I'm so relieved to have found you guys.'

'I'm glad you did. Any cricket fan is welcome here. Tell you what, if you feel up to it, we're going to have a bit of a knock around in the nets; we've got a big game coming up tomorrow.'

'Normally I'd love to, but I'll come and watch if that's okay. I'm still feeling a bit shaky.'

'Well, whatever, there's no pressure. See how you feel. The rest of us, however, need to get down there.'

In the nets, practice was already underway. WG was facing a steady stream of bowling from a line up of enthusiastic bowlers. Thommo and Fred were sending down some of their quick stuff, while Ranji provided a subtle variation with his off spin. Beaky was waiting to one side padded up.

'Watcha, Beefy. Who's this lanky lad?'

Beefy joined him and introduced Mikey.

'How's the practice session going?'

'Not bad, there's a not much troubling WG; he's so solid in defence.'

At that moment, the bearded WG bludgeoned a slow ball tossed up by Ranji into the net.

'He's not too bad on the attack either,' Beaky observed.

Fred was next up. Fired up by the dismissive attitude WG had showed Ranji's bowling, he hurtled in off his long run. He approached the wicket, collected himself in his delivery stride and unleashed a sickeningly fast ball. WG was up to it and shouldered arms, allowing the ball to pass speedily but safely past him.

'Is that all you've got?' WG taunted him.

'Uh oh, that won't go down well,' Beaky observed nervously.

Sure enough, by the time Fred had collected the ball and made it back to the end of his mark, it was clear he wouldn't be holding anything back. Again he roared in. This time, as he released the ball, Fred let out a yelp and fell away, clutching his shoulder. WG gently trapped the relatively tame delivery that had arrived at his end.

Beefy ran to his aid.

'Are you okay?'

'I've put my shoulder out,' Fred moaned. 'That's done it now. What about the match?'

'C'mon, mate, let's get you to Mrs Heyhoe. I'm sure it's not that bad.' But the look on Beefy's face as he glanced back at Beaky suggested that he wasn't convinced.

Meanwhile, the Pest Arrest crew were circling the

neighbourhood doing their rounds. Stan had been disappointed by the lack of texts of doom received on their mobile phones from the MILK machine. Bob, however, was starting to take a slightly more philosophical view on the role of technology in their line of work.

'I hate it when the gadgets don't work,' Stan sulked.

'But surely this is a struggle between man and beast.'

'Naa, mate.'

'Where is the thrill of the hunt when you rely solely on technology?'

'The thrill comes when I get home at a reasonable time,' Stan countered.

'But our hunting instincts focus on discovery, tracking and capture. The excitement of returning home with the prize, maybe of even hanging it on your wall.'

'I'm not hanging any dead mouse on my wall.'

'But man is programmed to hunt for food or to hunt for predators that pose a danger to him.'

'Listen, David Attenborough, I'll be posing a danger to you if you keep wittering on.'

'Stanley, you're a philistine.'

'That may be true. Now let's get in there and zap the little critters.'

The van had pulled up outside the old sorting office.

'You know what? You're getting soft,' Stan reprimanded his colleague. 'What this outfit needs is a bit of vim and vigour. I should have your job.'

'Well, at the moment, I have my job, so you go and get the stuff out of the back of the van.'

The two men got out of the van equally nosily to make their own points. Stan went to the back of the van and Bob to the front of the building to disarm the alarm. As he fumbled with the keys at the front door, he could have sworn he heard a scuffling sound coming from below him. He went to the edge of the stairwell and looked down. There at the foot of the stairs was a neat circle of rats who appeared to be playing a game. Bob shook his head for a moment and looked again.

'Oi, Stan, come and pinch me.'

'You what?' said Stan, staggering up under a load of equipment.

'Look at that, mate.'

For a moment, the two men stood spellbound before Stan shouted.

'Don't just stand there, GET 'EM!'

The two men lumbered down the stairs, and in an instant, the rats were gone. Stinger had taken the bat and Spotty the stump and all that remained was a hazel nut rolling and spinning on its axis.

The rats' practice may have been interrupted, but back at Lord's, things were being ramped up a notch. Under the Long Room, Mrs Heyhoe had applied a poultice to Fred's sore shoulder. He'd have to take things easy, but he wasn't ruled out of the game completely. He was wearing a sling and feeling sorry for himself.

'You'll be fine,' Beefy encouraged him. 'A good night's sleep, and you'll be firing on all cylinders tomorrow.'

As they walked down the corridor, Compo scampered up.

'You have to come and see this,' he said breathlessly.

While Bob and Stan were staring disbelievingly at one sight nearby, the mice were doing the same down at the cricket net.

The practice session had been in full swing when Mikey announced, 'You know what, I'm feeling much better. Do you think I could have a bowl?'

Don had been having a bat, and the withering barrage that was unleashed on him was the talk of the colony.

Mikey had taken a ball and paced out a mark. Once in position, he started a relaxed run up. He dipped his head in a little nod in the middle of it before gliding in to the wicket. A swishing sound accompanied him, his feet barely seeming to touch the ground. A fluent, graceful action generated a frightening pace.

From the other end, Don watched the ball from beneath his conker helmet. Mikey bowled the ball. Don saw it leave his hand. It pitched a little over halfway up the wicket. Don edged forward and hung his bat out in line with the ball. It was at this point that the ball seemed to vanish. It had deviated just the tiniest fraction from the straight, in that moment beating the bat. Almost instantly the sound of Don's off stump being rattled followed. If ever a ball was unplayable, that was it.

From then on, Mikey continued to bowl the fastest spell anyone had witnessed. Don had a breather and Gatt swallowed hard, taking his place. As Don left the net, a little group gathered round him.

'That was phenomenal!' said Beefy.

'Not quite what I was thinking,' Don sighed as he wiped a bead of perspiration from his brow.

'We've got to include him in our starting line up, surely?'

WG had hit the nail on the head. But it would mean that someone would have to step down from the team.

'Is there any way we can squeeze him into the team? What about Fred, isn't he injured?'

'Mrs Heyhoe seems to think it's just a minor strain, and that as long as he's sensible, he'll be fine for a one-off game. His experience is invaluable, and you know what he's like keeping everybody on their toes in the field.'

They all knew Beefy was right.

'We'll put it to a vote then,' Don proposed.

'No need, I'll drop out,' volunteered Bumble. 'I'll be the umpire; I've always wanted to give it a go. Just so long as someone can find me a nice white coat.'

So it was decided. Mikey would join the team, and Bumble would officiate. The practice resumed and throughout the mouse residence preparations for their win-at-all-costs game continued relentlessly.

Chapter Ten

In London that evening, the England players were tucked up in their hotel. They'd enjoyed a successful day. There was much to look forward to with Joe Root on the verge of a double hundred and Australia in a vulnerable position.

Elsewhere things were a little more unsettled. Compo had slipped away from the team practice for some quiet time to himself. He'd made his way up through the walls to a spot on the first balcony of the pavilion. He sat himself directly behind the test match wicket. Opposite him the Media Centre looked back at him like an unblinking cyclops. Together, he and it surveyed the immaculate playing area. The test wicket dead centre, covered for the night, and the ghostly sandy rectangles of used wickets either side of it. He did a visual tour of the stands that he knew so well. This was his home. Surely he couldn't lose this.

But Don and Beaky had got together to discuss 'worst-case scenarios.' To their minds, there was every chance that the mice would have to relocate. They agreed that the best option open to them was probably the lawnmower shed. But it was at the Nursery End of the ground. Trying to get the little ones there would be a major undertaking. They'd have to leave most of their possessions and start again. It was a bleak prospect.

Fred was nowhere to be seen. He'd taken himself off to bed to rest his shoulder. Knotty had nipped out and pulled some of the stuffing out of a cushion to make his bed nice and cosy for him. As long as he didn't stiffen up overnight, the chances were he'd be fine. Everyone knew that he was a bit of a drama queen and liked a bit of fuss made of him.

At the cricket net, Mikey was due a bat. As he sat padded up, he watched his new friends who'd been so welcoming. Despite this, he was a bit lonely and felt a bit out of place. He missed the comforts of his own home. He wondered about his parents and brothers and sisters. What would they be up to right now? One thing was for sure, they'd be worried and missing him.

Mrs Heyhoe and some of the other ladies were hard at work sewing. Some weeks ago, she'd been brought a length of blue material by one of the scavengers. She'd had an idea for it then, but with the advent of the big match, she'd been spurred on. On the floor near them a line of mouselets were lined up hard at work painting a banner on a length of bandage.

Everyone was keen to contribute to the team effort to overcome the threat to their home.

In his home, McCrackers sat surrounded by cricket-inspired paintings and memorabilia. A lifetime in cricket had made him a tiny bit fanatical. Despite having watched it all day, even now he was contemplating the day's events and Root's score. A significant milestone was an exciting event for any young cricketer. Whether it be in a Sunday friendly match on a village green or in a test match at Lord's. He remembered his own maiden first class century. It had been a hard-fought knock against Yorkshire. He'd got the yellow covered Wisden Cricketers' Almanack for 1962 down off the shelf.

Wisden, the 'Bible of Cricket', a cricket reference book published once a year. The book fell open at a well-thumbed page. He read the entry detailing that match, picturing the day in his mind's eye. It seemed as though it had happened just yesterday. He closed the book with a sigh, his youth and his fitness left within its pages.

Bob from Pest Arrest was reading too. He'd received a job application form from Hiber Nation Animal Sanctuary for the post of assistant carer. It was a bit of a step down from his lead role at Pest Arrest. However, he'd take it if they offered it to him. He needed a brighter horizon to his day instead of the death and destruction he dealt out. Stanley would be delighted to hear the news and the promotion it would bring. In Bob's view, he was welcome to it.

Whoever was in the role at Pest Arrest, the rat's precarious way of life would continue until they could establish a new permanent home. Although he rarely showed it, the responsibility of being the boss weighed heavily on Bristles. The game would be a piece of cake, and the mice would have to leave. He'd made his mind up about that. There was the nagging concern about its suitability. Rats and humans in such close proximity would be difficult. They weren't as good as the mice at covering their tracks, and once onto their scent, the humans would make life pretty uncomfortable for them. What he did know, however, was that he'd be delighted to leave the metal box that they currently called home. Any time anyone moved, the whole thing seemed to clang, and none of them had had a decent night's sleep since they moved in.

Stinger was also on edge. He was competitive by nature, and he wanted his teammates to give a good account of themselves in the match. As he saw it, their strength lay in their batting. Hopefully they'd win the toss, bat first and pile on the runs. Bristles would undoubtedly be crucial to their success as a batsman. But a batsman only gets one shot. He only had to make one mistake. It might only take one good ball and then... what was the phrase? 'One wicket brings two'. He shook his head, trying to banish the thought from his mind.

Their bowling would a bit of a lottery. No doubt they'd give away plenty of extras. Wides and the odd beamer, or high full toss had been a particular problem in their practice. Rags' spin had been a surprise discovery, and if things got out of control, he could bowl himself at one end and Rags at the other. The team's fielding would take care of itself as long as everyone kept on their toes. There was bound to be the odd mistake, but the opposition would make them too. They'd even each other out. But there is a tendency for the concentration of a part-time fielder to wander. Stinger would have to be a firm captain, but trying to give a group of rats orders was going to be tricky to say the least.

Meanwhile, while some wrestled with their

innermost thoughts, Spotty was dreaming about whether the moon was really made of cheese.

Chapter Eleven

Day Four of the Ashes second test

There is a great film called 'Goal' about the England victory in the 1966 World Cup final. The film starts with a man called Mr McElroy wearily making his way up some steps. When he gets to the top, he unlocks an ordinary-looking door with a small key. Behind the door is Wembley Stadium, a vast empty, echoey space. Later that day, it will be the backdrop for arguably the most memorable moment in British sport.

It seems unlikely that there is small, ordinary-looking door that opens Lord's Cricket Ground. Between you and me, I think there is someone there twenty-four hours a day. For the sake of nostalgia, let's pretend that Mr Hobbs had opened the ground that day with one small key. He enjoyed making a circuit of the ground early in the morning when he had the place to himself. Soon the ground would come to life. That was the crucial element. The ingredient that made Wembley on that day in 1966 had been the people.

At various points outside the ground, the MCC members and ticket holders had queued and waited to be let in. While the spectators had arrived on time, it seemed that London had made a sluggish start. It was Sunday after all and a hazy overcast morning. Surely even one of the world's most vibrant cities was entitled to a day off. Really, it was just slow to get going, and by lunchtime, some of the bustle would return. Once upon a time it would have been a rest day in the test, but times had changed. At the weekend, if you didn't have a ticket, then you wanted to be able to watch the match in HD on your mega TV. But if you did have one, then it provided an extra day for families to see the cricket together.

Inside the ground, talk was of whether the young England opening batsman would go on to make his double century. Would England declare? Did Australia have the nerve and cheek to save the game or even win?

McCrackers was back at the ground. He'd given up hopping the previous evening when, after half an hour, he'd still failed to hail a taxi. He was in good form, tipping his hat to everyone he knew and a number of Australian visitors he didn't.

The match had got under way without any mouse support. They hadn't missed much as the two young

English batsmen got off to an unpromising start. One had tripped over the boundary rope on his way to the wicket, and four overs later it was all over. There had been a six, a wicket, a dropped catch and then a mistimed trick-shot. There was to be no 200, and the England captain put everyone out of their misery by declaring. So leaving Australia the small matter of scoring 583 runs to win.

The mice were woken somewhat unexpectedly by Spiff. He'd found a direct route into the ground through the sewer system. It had brought him out in the gents' beneath the Allen Stand. From there, he'd had a risky dart across the tarmac before entering the building through the drain under the pavilion. He followed the pipe that led up to the 'thunderbox' and passed into the world beneath the Long Room unchallenged.

The main corridor of the mouse residence was deserted. Spiff swept round it, sniffing out its residents. He stuck his snout into a dark dormitory. Thommo was sleeping soundly in the bed nearest the door. Spiff reached in and gave him an unsympathetic shake.

'Holy Dooley, mate! Whatzup?' Thommo woke with a start.

In the dark dormitory, Spiff was outlined in the

door. The natural oils in his coat caught the light from the corridor, giving him a shiny golden outline as he filled the doorway. For Thommo, waking from deep sleep, he presented a truly horrific sight.

'K-k-keep away!' Thommo stuttered, backing into his bed and pulling some of the bedding fluff up to protect him.

'Sss... illy little mousey,' he hissed. 'It's Spiff, Bristles' associate.' He clicked the last syllable out with his tongue. 'Go and get daddy, little boy.'

Thommo scrambled out of bed. Now he was awake, and Spiff had pushed his buttons. He was in no mood to be bullied further.

'First of all you can get out of here,' he gave Spiff a good shove in the tummy to get him to back into the corridor, '... and wait, yer ding bat.'

With that, Thommo trod on Spiff's tail as hard as he could before scampering off to get Don and Beefy.

When the three of them returned, they found that Spiff had raided their larder and was helping himself to everyone's breakfast.

'Delicious,' he said, licking his lips. 'No doubt you'll be leaving all this for us, as you won't be able to a carry it.'

'What do you want?' Beefy challenged him. 'We weren't expecting to see you lot until later.'

'Yeah later, that's why Bristles sent me. When exactly do you want us?'

'Come to the 'thunderbox' after ten o'clock this evening. We will have everything ready. There are three churches near here, and their clocks chime every hour. Because of the traffic, you don't normally hear them, but at ten you will. Count the number of rings, and we will expect you sometime after that.' Don gave the orders with authority.

Some of the other mice had been woken and had joined the group. Now it was Spiff's turn to feel uncomfortable. He was outnumbered and taken aback by the little mouse's confidence. He edged backwards away from them.

'After ten, I've got that. See you later, *losers!*' he blurted before turning tail and disappearing.

'Now we're up, I reckon we ought to see what's happening in the cricket,' Beefy suggested, and the others agreed.

The mice were delighted to find that at lunch, the Aussies had lost three wickets and still had a mountain to climb. By the time they reached their vantage point, the Australians were showing a bit of resistance. The No.3 batsman and the Australian captain were both well on their way to half centuries and had just stopped for a drinks break.

Mr Hobbs was following the Australians' progress with mixed feelings. He'd started the day fully expecting the match to go into a fifth day as scheduled. A succession of quick wickets and a missed stumping suggested that the game would be over long before that. It was always a shame when matches didn't run their full course, but this wasn't altogether a bad thing if you were the clerk of works. With a hectic schedule, being handed an extra day to tick things off his 'to-do list' was a bonus. He could get the guys from Pest Arrest in. They could clear away whatever there might be to clear away. He shuddered at the thought—rather them than he.

Then the tempo of the game changed. The Australians slowly started to turn things round. Mr Hobbs' outlook changed again. The match would go into a fifth day after all; he'd go back to his original plan. Then, as the cricketing rollercoaster edged to safety, it suddenly plunged again as three wickets fell for 3 runs. Australia were up against it once again.

Twenty runs later, their last two recognised batsmen were back in the 'hutch' too. That was it as far as Mr Hobbs was concerned. He'd call Pest Arrest now and schedule them for some time the next day.

The mice were to-ing and fro-ing too. They'd stuck with it, believing an England victory was imminent, and then the last three Australian batsmen managed to add another 73 runs together. The umpires allowed more time and still they hung on. The last two batsmen had made it to the last over of the day. One string bean and one burly bowler, each one resolute in defence or nudging the occasional single. Everyone in the ground sucked in a breath, resigned to the fact that the match would have to be settled the next day. Then, with three balls left to bowl, the tenth wicket fell, leaving Australia 347 runs short. Out of 35 matches between the two countries at Lord's, it was only the 7th England had won.

With the late finish, the mice had stayed out longer than they'd planned. There was quite a lot to organise before this game, and they needed to get back home as quickly as possible.

Their usual mode of transport from their vantage point, the food lift, was out of order. With the building still full of people, this meant they'd have to make the entire journey beneath the plaster of the walls. It was a dark and dirty passage, but entirely safe. They followed each other down, snaking their way through the old lath and plaster down two floors. They emerged, led by Beefy, at the entrance to their home. The mice helped each other and patted each other down.

Mrs Heyhoe was waiting for them with Mrs Gatt and Mrs Beaky in attendance.

'I'm glad to see you're not going to walk all that dust in here.'

'We wouldn't dream of it, Mrs H', Beefy said with a grin.

'Where have you lot been? We've all been getting anxious; there's quite a lot of stuff to move you know.'

Mrs Gatt and Mrs Beaky nodded in agreement.

Mrs Heyhoe was right. As well as the scoreboard, there were a number of lengths of string for the boundary. Bumble's chefs' hats had been rejected as unsuitable, much to his disgust. Some tea-light candles, Willow's specially made stumps and their other cricket equipment. It all had to be moved upstairs so that when the coast was clear, they could move it into place.

'We've put out a snack for everyone to keep us going. So I think we should get down to the canteen for that now.'

At the end of the corridor they found the youngsters already lined up nibbling their rations. They were excitable and giggly.

'How many runs are you going to get, Compo?' asked Squeaker, one of Bumble's boys.

'It isn't all about one person, it's a team effort, Squeaker.'

The young mouse looked a bit downcast at this put down, but Compo hadn't intended it.

'Fifty at least,' he added with a wink.

While the mice had their meal, the end-of-match presentation was taking place on the outfield in front of the pavilion. Everyone seemed to be in a bit in a hurry. The extra time allowed by the umpires had played havoc with the TV schedules, while the players seemed anxious to get off to make the most of their suddenly acquired day off. The interviews concluded and the handshakes made, the two teams drifted away to their respective dressing rooms. Three of the England players were walking through the Long Room in a group. They were in high spirits, and one of them had been awarded the 'Man of the Match' medallion.

'Let's have a look,' said one.

'He wants a look because he knows he'll never get one himself,' joked another.

'Take care of it,' the medal winner instructed.

But seconds later the medal was rolling across the floor and under the radiator cover at the end of the room. It arrived just as the mice were moving all their bits and bobs from under the floor to this staging post. From here, when the time came, they could literally just push everything out onto the Long Room floor.

Gatt had just struggled up with one of the tea-lights as the medal rolled in.

Beaky and Compo were already there manhandling the scoreboard.

'Look at this, guys,' he whispered, steadying the medal. 'This would make a great trophy.'

No sooner had he spoken than a huge hand was thrust into the space. The mice pressed themselves against the wall as it swept around, searching for the medal. Gatt held out the medal and eventually the hand found it. He gently nudged it into the fingers, and the hand withdrew.

'Did you find it okay?'

'Yeah, but it was weird. I could have sworn something handed it to me.'

'Hmmm… of course it was 'handed' to you,' his teammate replied sarcastically.

He dismissed his misgivings with a shrug and joined the other cricketers as they passed through the door. The rattle of their boot studs and laughter filtered away as they disappeared up the stairs to the home dressing room.

Now the mice would have to wait. Slowly the building would empty. The Lord's staff would move in and do their chores. McCrackers, the self-appointed custodian, would do his rounds, and then they'd have the place to themselves.

So the hours passed, and eventually the unmistakable thump of McCrackers' bat stick echoed round the building. The elderly man had reached the notice board area and was just on his way out. It had been a long day, and a lot of cake and cups of tea had been consumed. Before he set off on his journey home, he decided to make a pit stop in the washrooms in the basement.

As McCrackers disappeared down the stairs, a Lord's steward appeared brandishing a huge bunch of keys. He hadn't seen anybody as he toured the ground floor and was certain he had the place to himself. No sooner had McCrackers disappeared than the steward swept down the stairs. He had a quick look in the washroom and then firmly locked the door. McCrackers was situated in a cubicle blissfully unaware of this fact.

Five minutes later, he was studying his reflection in a mirror over the basins. He ran a hand through his beard and turned his head sideways.

'My, you're a fine-looking fellow, McCrackers,' he said, taking his walking stick and walking to the door.

At first he thought he just hadn't pulled hard enough. He tightened his grip and gave the door a yank. It didn't budge. He twisted the doorknob more urgently and pulled again.

'Locked,' he murmured. 'The damn thing's locked.'

He tried again, but it was useless.

'Hello, is anybody out there? I'm still in here! Can someone let me out, please?'

But by now the steward was outside the building and couldn't hear him.

He gave the door a good pounding with both his fists, but still there was no response.

'Curses,' said McCrackers, wishing that he'd attempted to get to grips with the mobile phone his daughter had given him for Christmas. It was still in its box at home.

High in one of the walls were two windows. He tottered over to them and attempted to reach one with his stick. He was about 10 centimetres short. He tried a small jump, but it was useless. He had a sudden brainwave and cradled his bat stick in his both hands before launching it in the air. It was a good throw and the bat stick made firm contact with the glass. There was a shattering of glass, and the stick passed straight through and out of sight.

'Ooer, I hadn't expected that to happen,' McCrackers mumbled to himself. But perhaps the noise would bring someone to investigate. There was a large packet of paper towels on the counter. He placed them up against the wall and sat down on them, but no one came. Time passed, and eventually the old boy dozed off.

He was still asleep when the church clocks south, west and east of the ground chimed in unison. The rats took their lead from it and threaded their way through a storm drain into the sewer system. Spiff led the way towards Lord's followed by his teammates, each of them carrying a piece of their make-do cricket equipment.

The church bells had also given the mice the signal to go up and set up the pitch. Don had settled on a spot in the middle of the Long Room. This way they'd benefit from the security lighting outside the building as well as the ever-glowing emergency lighting. Their tea-lights would give them the extra light they'd need.

The old room rose like a giant cavern above the mice, its walls soaked with the history of cricketing decades. The ghostly murmur of spectators and ripple of applause seemed ever-present. While the sombre faces of past cricket greats peered into the space frozen within their frames.

Don directed the proceedings.

'Willow, let's set one set of stumps here...'

Willow had constructed some special stumps set on little wooden planks to support them.

'...and Beefy if you'd care to do the honours.'

Beefy measured out twenty-two bat lengths and positioned the other set.

Knotty had a roll of white medical tape, and he and Compo stretched out a length. Beaky then nipped it off and together they stuck it to the floor a pace and a half from the stumps. They then repeated the process at the other end.

Thommo, WG and Ranji dragged the knotted pieces of string that formed the boundary rope into place, and Compo and Beaky pushed the scoreboard to the edge of it.

'Ooh, it's all coming together nicely,' Willow observed.

'Okay, everyone will need to grab a tea-light, and I'll get the book of matches,' Don ordered. The colony book of matches was a revered item, handled only in emergencies by Don.

'Once we've done that, then it's back home to wait for the opposition.'

When they got there, Bumble met them. He was proudly sporting his umpire's coat. Actually, it was more of a tabard made out of a white napkin, but he was pleased with the air of authority it gave him.

'Mrs Heyhoe wants to see us all before we go up; she's waiting with the other ladies down the corridor.'

The mice crowded down it in a little group and found Mrs Heyhoe in the middle of the other ladies, supported by the children.

Mrs Heyhoe stepped forward.

'We know that a lot depends on you boys this

evening. So hopefully to give you all a little boost, the ladies and I have been working on caps for the whole team. If each of you would like to come and collect one.'

Mrs Gatt stepped forward with a pile of blue caps, and Mrs Heyhoe handed one to each of the team.

Everyone had always admired Compo's in the past, and it was a nice for the team spirit that they now all had matching ones. They were all still complimenting each other on how splendid they looked when they were rudely interrupted.

'Oi, is this a fashion show or are we going to play this cricket match?'

It was Bristles leading his team up through the 'thunderbox'.

Don and Beefy stepped up to acknowledge them.

'I thought you'd chickened out,' Beefy said provocatively.

'We wouldn't have missed it for the world, choochiface.' Bristles tickled him under the chin condescendingly.

'Shall we get on with it?' Beefy seethed.

'We'd like nothing better.'

All the rodents made their way up to the Long Room and gathered at the side of the pitch.

'They've made a good job of it, I'll say that for them,' Spotty observed.

Bumble had just put the bails on the stumps. He cleared his throat.

'Ahem, as the umpire for the game, may I call the two captains together for the toss?'

Don and Bristles made their way out to the middle of the wicket.

'As the visitors...'

'Not for much longer,' Bristles sneered.

'As the visitors,' Bumble continued, 'would you like to call?'

'Tails seems appropriate,' he said with a cheesy grin.

'Righto.' Bumble heaved a five-pence coin into the air.

Everyone watched the coin turn end over end.

'Tails it is!' Bumble announced.

'Good, we'll have a bat,' Bristles said ominously.

Chapter Twelve

Mouse Cricket Club v The Rat Packers

'Oh, that's convenient that it's one of your blokes that's in charge. In the interests of fair play, we've brought our own referee along.'

'Umpire,' Beefy corrected.

'Umm... pire then,' Bristles chanted. 'Mr Cheese, would you join us?'

'It would be my pleasure, Bristles.'

'I *do* not like the look of him,' Beefy said to Don in a hushed voice that wasn't quite hushed enough.

'You two got a problem with that?'

'Not me,' Bumble interrupted. 'I'm sure we'll get along famously. How do you do?'

Mr Cheese said nothing, but eyed Bumble suspiciously.

Bumble pressed on anyway.

'What say we get the names of the teams down and make a start?'

CMJ had forgotten about his role as scorer. In fact, he'd had to be reminded about the whole game. At the last moment he'd appeared, completely flustered and full of apologies. He'd been waiting in the Committee Room thinking the match was in there. He had with him his prized possession, what appeared to be a proper notebook. In reality, it was an old diary that he'd trimmed down to mouse proportions with Willow's help. In it, he kept a record of cricket matches he'd watched. This evening's would certainly be one for his record book.

After some consultation and frenzied scribbling, the teams were agreed.

Mouse Cricket Club	The Rat Packers
Don (Capt)	Twitchy
WG	Scruffer
Beaky	Bristles
Gatt	Stinger (Capt)
Compo	Skunky
Beefy	Spotty (wk)
Knotty (wk)	Bitesize
Thommo	Long Tail
Ranji	Spiff
Fred	Fleabag
Mikey	Rags

The names of the two teams collected, Bumble was

keen to get the format of the game sorted.

'I suggest we play 20 overs a side if that's all right with you?' he ventured, tossing a red-painted match nut from hand to hand.

'Over the side?' Mr Cheese replied doubtfully.

'Each team has twenty overs of six balls to score as many runs as possible,' Bumble spelt things out.

Mr Cheese, who was only there in his role as 'general pain in the neck', pulled a face that suggested he didn't understand.

'I tell you what. All you need to worry about are run outs. Let me explain.' As the two umpires made their way out to the middle, Bumble described the technicalities of a run out.

While the rats padded up, the mice walked out to field. Fred was chomping at the bit, eager to bowl the first over and 'put the wind up them'. Don was more measured. He tossed the ball to Beefy and then set the field.

The Rat Packers' openers walked out to the wicket. Knotty behind the stumps liked to chat to the batsman.

'Those are pretty snazzy pads... yes, very snazzy. I wonder what you call them. Bubble pads I guess.'

Twitchy, who'd taken his stance to receive the first

ball, put his hand up to stop the bowler. He turned to Knotty.

'Are you going to keep that chatter up or am I going to have to...'

'Consider it zipped, chum,' he said with a grin.

But Twitchy wasn't composed. He fidgeted about the crease.

'Give them a battering,' Spotty called from the boundary.

'Play!' cried Bumble from his position behind the stumps at the bowler's end, and the action began.

Beefy polished the ball on his leg and started his run up for the first ball. Twitchy took a step towards him, then a step back. Beefy bowled and Twitchy swung the bat. He did a good impersonation of a windmill and was bowled first ball.

'HORRAY!' cried the mice in unison.

'BOOOOO!' howled the rats.

'He must have cheated. Go on, Mr Cheese, send him off,' Twitchy moaned.

But Twitchy was out, and he reluctantly trudged off the pitch. Compo marked a wicket down on the calendar, CMJ scribbled furiously in his book, and Bristles walked out to bat. There are times in cricket when it is better not to take a wicket. Keep a bad or 'out of nick' batsman in and dry up the runs. This was just such an occasion as Bristles strode to the wicket.

'Would you like a guard?' Bumble asked.

'You'll be needing a guard if you break my concentration. Just let him bowl, will you?'

'Wait a moment, left-hand bat,' Don observed and changed the field accordingly while Bristles tutted impatiently.

Beefy charged in again. As he'd done in practice, Bristles took one step down the wicket and drove the ball smartly back past the bowler. It was a confident start. The next ball fared no better, and Compo had marked off the first 8 days of January with just three balls bowled.

Knotty had remained tight-lipped. For the next ball, Beefy changed his grip. Bristles had a big swish at it, but it swung away from him at the last moment.

'Ooooh!' Knotty exclaimed.

Bristles turned and glared at him. Knotty pushed his cap more firmly on his head with both hands and crouched to receive the next ball without making eye contact.

But the fact that there was obviously more to this

game than he thought played on Bristles' mind. He missed the remaining balls of the over to the soundtrack of Knotty's theatrical gasps.

For the next over, Don called on Mikey. Fred butted in.

'No way, Don. I'm a senior member of the team; I should be on.'

'We need to look after you, Fred. We'll need your experience in the final overs.'

'Either I'm fit or not. Give us it here,' he ordered gruffly.

Fred took the ball and marched back to the end of his mark. Scruffer was facing the new bowler. Although Fred's bustling run up was intimidating, he managed to get some bat on the first ball.

'Run!' Bristles ordered.

The combination of Bristles against Fred was potentially explosive. Fred's first ball to him was a bouncer and whistled past Bristles' ears.

'Would you like a helmet?' Knotty chirped.

In response, the next short ball was sent sailing over the midwicket boundary. Bumble signalled a six with his arms in the air, and Knotty shut up. By the time he'd finished his over Fred was puffing a bit.

Bristles had added another couple of runs, but sharp fielding by the rest of the team had kept him pinned down.

Already the scoreboard read 17 for 1. Don and Beefy had a quick conversation between overs.

'We really need to keep that brute off strike,' Don warned.

'Leave it to me,' Beefy said grimly.

Beefy proceeded to fire in an over of 'yorkers', spearing in on Scruffer's toes. It had the desired effect. Scruffer managed to dig the ball out on each occasion, but failed to score. At the other end, Bristles was getting frustrated. He'd had a couple of false starts at a run, but had been sent back. On the fourth ball, Scruffer had just dabbed the ball halfway down the pitch in front of him. That was enough for Bristles, and he was off like a shot while Scruffer froze. With both the rats at one end, a run out looked certain. Everyone hesitated, then Bristles started to run back down the wicket. Scruffer started too, and Beefy joined in the fun. Beefy reached the ball, booted it between the two rat goalposts and scored in the top right-hand corner of the stumps.

After the rats grudgingly conceded that Scruffer

had been run out, Stinger joined Bristles.

'We need to make this partnership count, big guy.'

'If that fool had just legged it instead of hesitating, we'd have been fine.'

'Just don't take any unnecessary risks, got that?'

Very soon it was apparent to the mice that Stinger was a class above the others. He punched his first ball for two through the covers and then nicked a single off the last ball of the over. He worked the next over around the wicket while Bristles belligerently bashed the odd boundary.

As Fred started the sixth over, the total had moved on to 43 for 2. Once again Bristles was on strike, and their duel resumed. The first ball went for four, an ugly smear to square leg. Fred walked back to his mark seething and muttering to himself. However, he managed to restrain himself, and the next ball was a bit slower. Bristles wasn't expecting it, and as a result, he was through his shot a bit early. The ball caught him high on the bat and popped back to the bowler for the simplest of catches. Unfortunately, Fred wasn't expecting it either and having juggled the ball, he dropped it.

'Rats!' he cried in frustration, kicking at the ground.

'Oi, Umpire, that's sledging, isn't it?' Stinger asked Bumble.

'Frustration that's all, pure and simple.'

'Well, I think you should have a word, Ump.'

'Well, I think we should get on with the game.' Bumble looked over his shoulder to make sure Fred was back at the end of his run up. 'Play!' he called.

Fred came haring in, a fearsome sight, having ratcheted up his pace a notch. He delivered the ball.

'Neeargh!' he yowled as his damaged shoulder went again.

The ball nut rolled harmlessly to Bristles, who did his best to smash it into next week.

The mice gathered round Fred. It was clear he wouldn't be able to finish the over.

'Do you want to go off, Fred? I'm sure the opposition will lend us a fielder?'

'I wouldn't be so sure about that,' Stinger interrupted.

'You rotters,' snapped Don. It was unlike him to get ruffled.

'Don't worry, Don. I'll swap with Mikey at long leg.'

'Mikey, you'll have to finish the over anyway.'

'No problem, Don,' said Mikey as the lanky mouse

started to pace out his run up.

Compo crossed the pitch in front of Bristles.

'One down, ten to go,' Bristles chuckled.

'We'll see who's laughing in a minute,' Compo replied coldly.

With everyone back in position, Mikey started his relaxed run up, dipped his head halfway and then bowled. The difference in pace was significant and too good for Bristles. By the end of the over, he'd faced three balls and hadn't been able to lay a bat on any of them.

At the end of the over, Spotty ran out with a helmet made out of a single section of an egg box. Bristles swatted him away.

'Do you think I'm weak?' he snapped. But Bristles was rattled, and it showed.

Don and Beefy had another meeting.

'I think it's time to bamboozle our opponents, don't you?'

Beefy nodded and called Ranji over.

'Ho ho, this should be good,' Stinger muttered to himself as he saw what a short run up Ranji had. But it was a classic case of the 'tortoise and the hare' type of thinking.

Ranji bounded up to the wicket and delivered a looping slow ball. Stinger's eyes almost spun with delight at the prospect of a juicy slow full toss. But at the last moment, the ball dipped and beat Stinger's bat. The next ball was Ranji's off break, the next his 'doosra'. All three had completed confused Stinger, as Don had hoped. The only problem was that they'd also done for the wicketkeeper and with a long leg throwing in with his wrong arm, the rats had accumulated 6 byes. Six an over would take the rats to a formidable score. Knotty met Ranji halfway down the wicket for a conference.

'Sorry, mate, great bowling, but I just can't read what ball you're going to bowl.'

'I'll scratch my left ear for the off break, my right for the 'doosra', and nothing for my flipper.'

Knotty nipped back behind the stumps, and the over played out with 3 more dot balls.

The next two overs bowled by Mikey and Ranji were maidens. Stinger could play this waiting game, but it was driving Bristles mad. Now it was their turn to meet midwicket.

'Hit out or get out I say,' Bristles ordered aggressively.

'We can just keep the scoreboard ticking over. We

can accumulate with flicks, pushes and nudges.'

'Or bangs, biffs and boshes. Get back to your end and whack it.'

But Bristles had forgotten that the whacking would have to be at his end because he was still facing Mikey. He was as good as his word though, as he had a tremendous swish at the first ball. The ball caught the outside edge of his bat and flew through the slips for 4. The third caught the inside edge and narrowly missed the stumps before racing down to the boundary. At the end of the tenth over, the rats had progressed to 65 for 2.

Mrs Heyhoe and the mouse supporters arrived with drinks, and everyone had a break.

The two sides kept their distance as they discussed the state of the game.

'That skinny one is as quick as anything I've ever seen,' said Stinger, shaking his head.

'I think we're doing quite well,' Twitchy remarked.

'No thanks to you,' Bristles scolded.

'Yeah, out first ball of the game. What a twit,' Spiff agreed.

'Remember the team, guys,' Stinger urged.

While the rats squabbled, the mice were anxious

about the way things were going.

'That's not a bad score,' Beaky fretted. 'They've got runs on the board, and remember they're bigger and stronger than us. Runs are going to be hard to come by later.'

'We have to try and contain the big one.' Don expressed his concern.

'The other one is a good player too,' Beefy echoed it, which put the wind up everyone. If Beefy with all his self-belief was worried, then what hope was there for the rest of them?

After a drink, everyone went back to their positions and the game restarted. Up until now, Stinger had been so disciplined. He continued where he'd left off with his impenetrable forward defensive stroke against Ranji, but the drinks interval had broken his concentration. As Ranji ran in to bowl, he appeared to roll the ball in his fingers. Stinger saw this and, distracted, played down the wrong line. Ranji's 'doosra' turned like a leg break and clipped the bails.

'Whoop!' Knotty went up in celebration.

It was just the breakthrough the mice needed. There is a saying that one brings two, and sure enough, Skunky was no match for Ranji's cunning, and having been comprehensively beaten by his first ball, he spooned an easy catch to Compo at mid on second up.

This brought Spotty to the crease. He'd got himself into a bit of a muddle with his bubble-wrap protection. Anxious that Mikey didn't damage him, he appeared to be wearing boxing rather than batting gloves. However, he had a good eye for a ball and managed to get bat on ball and scramble a single.

Bristles was happy to get the strike and was keen to get the scoreboard moving again. He hoicked his first ball from Ranji to leg, but playing against the spin, the ball looped up in the opposite direction. Frustratingly for the mice, it fell in the middle of a group of fielders, and again the rats scrambled a single.

With Fred injured, Don had to find some overs from another bowler. Thommo would bowl some quick stuff towards the end of the innings. Gatt could bowl some of his medium pace 'wobblers', and he decided that now was a good time to bring him on.

'Oh my goodness, what have we here?' snorted Bristles.

But it was Gatt who had the last laugh. Gatt's 'wobblers' were so called because they did just that. He bowled the first ball, and Bristles tried to follow it.

Mesmerised by it wobbling through the air, he in turn wobbled his head to mimic its flight. As he did so, his headscarf loosened itself and dropped over his good eye. Unable to see, he wandered out of his crease and Knotty, having caught the ball, stumped him.

'Howzat!' the mice cried.

'Not out,' replied Mr Cheese.

'*What?*' Beefy exploded.

'You wouldn't want to take advantage of this poor rat and his *one* eye, would you now?' Mr Cheese replied smugly.

Bristles chuckled to himself as he bent down and picked the ball up. He knew he'd been way out of his ground. As he made to throw it to the bowler, WG bellowed from the boundary.

'Howzat!'

'Out,' Bumble replied simply. 'Out, handled the ball. On your way, son.'

Bristles was not happy, but sauntered off, dragging his bat behind him.

'You better make them pay for that,' he said to Bitesize as he passed him on his way to the wicket.

Bitesize did as instructed and, having survived the first couple of Gatt's deliveries, struck a couple of lusty blows to the boundary.

Don called on Thommo to bowl the next over. He walked up to the crease to start marking up his run and gave Bitesize the most searing look he could muster.

Bitesize turned towards his partner and waved Spotty over to him.

'Keep your wits about you; this little critter looks mean,' he advised.

Spotty swallowed hard and returned to his mark. Thommo took this as his cue and tore in before unleashing a slingshot ball at the unsuspecting Spotty.

Convinced that the ball was going to hit him between the eyes, Spotty dropped his bat and put his fists up in front of his face. The ball struck his bubble-wrap-bound hands and pinged off to the boundary.

With war declared, Thommo stomped back to the end of his run up. The next ball speared in. Spotty dropped to the ground much to the surprise of the wicketkeeper and four byes were added to the score. Spotty managed to survive the next three balls with a variety of unorthodox evasive actions. Eventually his luck ran out. The last ball sent the stumps cartwheeling, and Willow scurrying out to make quick repairs.

With the calendar scoreboard edging towards the

end of March at 83 for 6, Long Tail strode out to join Bitesize. Gatt was eager to bowl again given his success against Bristles. Unfortunately, Bitesize continued where he'd left off, dispatching two full tosses, albeit wobbling ones, for 4. The next delivery was pitched short and Bitesize rocked back in his crease and square-cut the ball, which was brilliantly stopped by Thommo. Sadly, his enthusiastic throw passed well over the head of the wicketkeeper and down to the boundary rope. The rats having run a single, the game's first 5 was registered. Long Tail was now on strike, and Gatt bowled a yorker to him—aimed at his toes. Long Tail jammed his bat down hard on the ball, unintentionally trapping his tail at the same time.

'YEEOUCH!' he let out an ear-splitting scream and hopped about holding his throbbing tail.

Mrs Heyhoe was called to administer first aid and a massive bandage was applied. It was clear that Long Tail wasn't keen to risk any more damage, so after a lot of fuss, it was agreed that he should 'retire hurt'.

Appropriately, the rats were now into the 'tail', as the bowling end of a batting line up is known. Bowlers not known for their skill with the bat could sometimes make an impact on the scoreboard by sheer brute force.

Spiff was definitely up for the challenge, and he bumped gloves with Bitesize as he joined him. Spiff's range of shots included the slog, the swish and the big yahoo, sometimes all three at once. But add a touch of coordination to this, and it was a dangerous mix as the 6 hit off the last ball of Gatt's over suggested.

The rats had scored nineteen off the over. It was a disaster for the mice, and the score was now over a hundred.

'I'm so sorry, Don,' Gatt apologised.

'Don't worry. Those overthrows could have happened to anyone. Thommo and Mikey can finish off for us now, which should slow them up a bit.'

Sure enough, the two fast bowlers were more than a match for the rats' tail-enders. Mikey bowled an unplayable maiden. Don had all his fielders well spread, and the flow of runs ground to a halt. Building pressure and frustration leads to rash decisions. Bitesize, trying to move the score on, skied a ball from Mikey. It went so high that several fielders, including Knotty, had congregated underneath it by the time it returned to earth.

'MINE!' they cried in unison.

'KEEPER'S!' boomed Beefy, overruling them, and

the wicketkeeper took it comfortably.

Fleabag's stay at the wicket was perhaps the shortest of the innings. He'd been watching Mikey from the boundary's edge and had no interest in sacrificing himself for the cause. In the end, as Mikey ran in to bowl, he dropped his bat and ran off waving his arms and shouting 'get me outta here!' and was stumped.

Rags joined Bitesize.

'Looks like we're the last two. Don't mess it up.'

It was hardly an inspirational greeting.

The juvenile rat appeared edgy and skittish as he took his guard.

'Start the car,' Bumble muttered under his breath, which implied that he didn't think it would take long for the next wicket to fall.

But despite the pace of Mikey's bowling, Rags looked surprisingly comfortable as he drove his first ball to mid-off. As he'd hit the ball in front of him, it was his call on the run.

'Yes!' he cried.

Bitesize set off like Usain Bolt. But Rags had struck the ball quite firmly, and it arrived at the fielder sooner than he'd expected.

Rags changed his call to 'Wait!' which he quickly

adjusted to 'No!' and then…

'Sorry!' as Bitesize was run out.

It was an innings that had gone this way and that. At times the rats had looked incompetent, and at times as if they'd amass a colossal total. If interviewed in post-match 'interview speak', Don would have said: 'That at the end of the day (insert commentator's name) if you'd offered us that at the start of the game, we'd have taken it' or some such pithy comment.

The Rat Packers were 102 for 9 with Long Tail retired hurt. The rats had not used all their overs, which was always going to hurt them. With a short break between innings, it would soon be time to see how the mice would do in reply.

Chapter Thirteen

In the pavilion basement, McCrackers had been woken. His paper-towel cushion had leant one way and deposited him on the floor. Although it had been a warm day, below ground, it had gotten cold, and he'd stiffened up. The old boy got to his feet in instalments. First straightening and arm, then a leg, a bend of the knee and then an impossible stretch to reach the door handle. With it firmly grasped, he put in a final momentous effort to haul himself to his feet. The entire process was punctuated with weight-lifter-like panting and a fantastic chorus of 'oohs' and 'ahhs'.

McCrackers shambled over to the basins and clicked on the vanity light. His reflection made him start visibly, and he did his best to smooth down his wayward hair and straighten his clothes. He collected his thoughts and looked around him. The only obvious aid to hand was the paper towel dispenser, and he gave the white metal box a half-hearted rattle. To see what he might use to dismantle it, he emptied his pockets onto the counter. A pair of tortoise-shell spectacles, a retractable silver toothpick, his club membership card, a conker on a string. Three cellophane wrapped toffees, a blue spotty handkerchief, his house keys on a bat-shaped key fob, some change and half a pencil. A motley collection of bits and bobs, but one that might have its uses.

For starters, he unwrapped one of the toffees and sucked it noisily. As he rolled it about his mouth, he inspected the paper towel holder whilst simultaneously humming in the style of a military band. At the bottom of the metal dispenser was a slot for a key—a simple latch to keep the refill compartment secure rather than a full-blown security feature. He took his house keys and managed to select one that slotted in part way. It was enough, and soon he was taking the whole appliance to pieces. A slim piece of metal about the size of a school ruler was one useful component, as was a wooden roller. He added them to his collection.

Next he prowled about the room looking for any way out. The windows were too small and too high anyway, even for a fit person to access. He'd have to find a way out through the door. After he'd examined it, it didn't seem quite such a crazy idea. The hinges had a pin with a rounded top slotted into them. If this pin were to be removed, then the hinge would split in two.

One half would remain attached to the door and the other the doorframe. His two new tools would be perfect for this, and he set to work driving the slim piece of metal under the rounded head of the pin. It was a good idea in principle, but his tools were not strong enough for the job. Time and again the metal bent, and in the end, he gave up.

In frustration, McCrackers gave the door handle another tug. Still stuck fast. He formed a gun with two fingers and blew the lock away with imaginary gunshots. In the movies things were always so simple. But wait a minute... the movies. What was that film he'd watched the other day? 'Mission Insufferable' was it? In that, the cool guy had unlocked a door with a coat hanger and a nail file. In his mind, he was every inch the hero; he had the necessary hardware and plenty of time to experiment.

He surveyed his tools. He rolled the toothpick in his hands. It was an Edwardian antique, his father's, so of great sentimental value, but it was perfect for the job. He'd need another sliver of metal. There was bound to be something in the towel dispenser, and soon he'd found a long blunt pin with a loop at one end.

He returned to the door, and as the hero in the film

had done, he inserted the pin into the bottom of the lock. This stopped the lock's cylinder turning and allowed him to slide in the toothpick. In a lock, there are a number of pins that if pushed up allows the mechanism to turn. To unlock the door, this was all that McCrackers had to do—push these pins up with his probing toothpick.

Unfortunately, he didn't know that. His method would rely on trial and error. A frustrating series of hopeful-sounding clicks as he worked on the lock. Eventually, if luck was on his side, he might stumble on the sequence that would unlock the door.

Chapter Fourteen

The Mouse Cricket Club's Innings

There was a lot of excitement as the mice prepared to bat. The children had come up to support the adults. It hadn't seemed wise when the rats were batting, as there was a group of them hanging around. Now, however, they were all safely in the field hurling a ball about between them.

The children had proudly unrolled their banner that read 'Mouse Cricket Club we ♥♥you' in slightly splurgy printing. Willow had pushed her latest creation into place. She'd been hard at work constructing a gate for the players to walk through. They had no fence, but the gate lent a certain formality to the proceedings, and she'd carved the inspirational words 'Walk to Glory' on the top bar.

Don and WG had finished padding up and, having been given a hug by their respective families, they made their way through the gate and out to the middle.

'Will you take the first ball or shall I?' asked WG.

'I think I will; we wouldn't want you out first ball. A number of those little guys have come to see you bat.'

WG preened his beard with pride.

'Do you really think so?'

'I know so. Now, let's get stuck into this lot and show them what we're made of.' Don was at full of encouragement.

As the two mice passed between Spiff and Long Tail in the outfield, it seemed that the difference in their size was magnified. Although the comparison between the well-fed pavilion dwellers and the scrawny street scavengers was actually not as bad as it might have been. However, Bristles was a big fellow, and he wandered over to welcome them to the wicket.

'Come and join our little party, gentlemen. Who's going to be the first victim?' He rubbed his hands together gleefully.

The batsmen did their best to ignore him and walked to their respective ends. Behind the umpire at the non-striker's end, Stinger was giving Spiff a last-minute coaching session. He was desperately trying to get him to remember to roll his arm over rather than chuck the ball.

'Remember that phrase we made up. Say it to yourself as you run in—to bowl is the goal, a chuck makes them duck!'

Spiff mouthed the words as if he was a robot obeying an order.

'That's it, now give 'em hell!' Stinger patted him on the back and sent him back to his bowling mark.

'Middle please, Bumble.' Don took his guard.

'Right arm over, six to come,' Bumble announced the bowler's action and got the innings off to a start.

Spiff ran into the wicket chanting his motto in his head, 'to bowl is the goal...'

As Stinger had feared, he threw the ball instead of bowling it.

An action that was shortly followed by a resounding, 'NO BALL!' bellowed by Bumble.

The spectators cheered, and CMJ licked his pencil, entering the first run in his book.

Out on the pitch, Don nodded to WG and smiled. At least they were off the mark.

Stinger had another consultation with Spiff. There was lots of gesticulating, and Spiff mimed a legal bowling action. Eventually he was ready again, and he started what was this time a rather slow and deliberate run up. Eventually he got to the crease, overran it and bowled the ball.

'NO BALL!' Bumble yelled a second time.

There was another consultation, after which Spiff cut the run up out of his bowling altogether. Much to Stinger's relief, and the rest of the team's surprise, this had the desired effect. Spiff managed to bowl a legal ball, which beat Don perhaps as much from the element of surprise than skill. What he did find was that with Spiff's extra height, the ball had bounced much more than he was used to. This meant it would be more difficult to play a forward defensive stroke. He'd have to play off the back foot, and he practiced his range of shots as the ball was returned to the bowler. As a result, he was up on his toes for the next ball and dabbed it into the leg side for a single. WG was now on strike. He prowled round the crease scratching a mark, prodding the pitch and finally casting an eye around the surrounding fielders.

'Could we get on with it?' Bristles enquired from the slips.

WG settled over his bat, Spiff bowled, and WG cut the ball hard so that it flashed through the slip cordon. Bristles took evasive action, and the ball ran down to the boundary.

'Happy now?' WG asked the rats' captain.

Bristles muttered something under his breath.

'I'd like to see you do that again,' Spotty goaded him from behind the stumps.

But WG was not going to be tempted into anything rash. Spiff, having got a couple of balls in the right place, was gaining in confidence. By bringing his shoulder over sharply, he was upping his pace, and the wise mouse was happy to defend until he'd got his eye in.

It was clear to Stinger that the two mice knew what they were doing. He had to credit himself with the fact that he was the rats' best bowler so he decided to take the next over.

Both the mice were surprised by the quality of Stinger's bowling. Even Bumble complimented him on his first ball, which pitched and left Don, making him play and miss. But actually, when someone bowls properly, it is sometimes easier to play proper cricket shots than it is to bowling that is wayward and unpredictable. As a result, the mice were able to rotate the strike, taking singles off each ball of the rest of the over.

'I thought you were supposed to be good,' Bristles challenged Stinger uncharitably as they crossed for the next over.

The mice had met for a midwicket conference.

'We need just over 5 runs an over, so we're up with the run rate,' said Don.

WG nodded and the two punched gloves. However, for all his fighting talk, Don was clearly feeling the pressure of his role in the team. He desperately wanted to play a 'captain's innings', but the more he wanted it, the worse things got.

Spiff bowled the third over, and to start with, Don couldn't get him away. He ended up fending off the short-pitched bouncy bowling more in self-defence than attack. Eventually he got a tickle on one down the leg side and the batsmen swapped ends.

'Hello, Granddad, nice to see you again,' Bristles started up from the slips. 'I thought you'd be using your bat as a walking stick.'

Inside his gloves, WG tensed the grip on his bat handle. 'Granddad, eh?' He'd show him. It is never a good idea to have a premeditated shot. Always better to play a ball on its merits. Despite this, WG was determined to repeat his earlier shot and send a howitzer in Bristles' direction.

Spiff bowled short, WG cut the ball, but just a smidge later than before. The ball rocketed off the face of the bat straight into Bristles' stomach.

"OUFF!' he took the full force of the shot.

Spotty ran to his aid while the mice set off on a run. Bristles got to his feet, clutching his tummy.

'Are you all right, mate?' Spotty asked.

'More than all right,' Bristles beamed as he held up the ball that he'd clutched to himself. 'You're out, Beardy!' he jabbed a thumb towards the gate on the boundary.

Don couldn't believe it and leant on his bat as he watched WG pass Beaky on his way out to the wicket.

Beaky took his guard and faced his first ball from Spiff. It was the second to last ball of the over, and he 'shouldered arms' to it, letting the ball pass harmlessly into the keeper's gloves. His next ball was almost identical, but he stepped to the offside slightly and pulled it through midwicket effortlessly.

'Nice shot,' Don beamed as they met.

'You'd expect nothing else from your number 3, would you?'

Don looked at the scoreboard showing 16 for 1. He'd hoped for a better start, but there was still plenty of time, and they had wickets in hand. Facing Stinger was a real test, and he was struggling to keep him out let alone score. The third ball of the next over beat him completely. As it passed him, the ball flicked something and went through to the wicketkeeper. Spotty caught the ball and asked the umpire.

'How was that?'

Bumble thought for a minute. Had Don edged the ball and been caught? No, his bat was well away from his pad. His pad, it had hit his pad. Plumb in front too. That meant he was out leg before wicket, so reluctantly he put his finger up.

Don's shoulders slumped. He couldn't believe it. The day he needed to play the innings of his life, and he'd let everyone down.

On the boundary, his teammates tried to make light of things, praising his effort and commitment. He'd have nothing of it and took himself to one side for a moment to gather his thoughts.

Gatt had already taken strike in the middle and was doing his best to be as aggressive in his approach as possible. It was a brave attitude, and he'd been hit quite hard in the chest having advanced down the wicket to Stinger's next ball.

'Don't rub it,' he muttered to himself. 'Show them no weakness.'

Therefore, it was great delight that the full face of

his bat met with the middle of the next ball. Timed to perfection, the ball sped to the mid-on boundary. Then he had a bit of luck with a 'Chinese' or 'Surrey' cut, an inside edge which narrowly missed the stumps. The ball was stopped by Fleabag on the boundary, but not before he and Beaky had run two.

The next over brought a change in the bowling. Stinger was keen to employ his secret weapon in the form of Rags, the leg spin bowler. This suited Beaky, who backed himself against spin. Gatt was happy too, the area under his arm was still tender, and he was keen not to take another blow there.

The change in pace accelerated the run rate, and the two batsmen took it in turn to flay Rags' bowling. But the slower ball had to be hit harder, and much to the frustration of the batsmen, the fielders were stopping the boundaries. However, they'd run hard, and ten off the over was a good return.

It had been quiet for a while, but Bristles decided that it was time for him to get involved again. Despite the fact that Stinger had tied up one end and was putting considerable pressure on the batting side, Bristles convinced him that he could keep this pressure up and took over.

'I'll get these two jumping around, just you watch,' he threatened as he took the ball and marched back to his mark.

'This should be interesting,' Spotty confided in Gatt, who was on strike.

No one could fault Bristles for effort, but sometimes his overconfidence was misplaced. He proceeded to bowl a selection of wides, no balls and a donkey-drop full toss that Gatt biffed for six. In the end, it took him ten balls to finish the over. He'd actually bowled two more wides at the end of the over, but Bumble couldn't take any more and didn't call them.

With the score on a respectable 45 for 2, Rags started a new over. He'd got his line and length sorted and was really giving the ball a good rip. So far, Gatt had managed to smother the spin by stretching out to the pitch of the ball. Then out of nowhere, Rags bowled what can only be described as a 'wonder ball'. Drifting to the leg side, Gatt followed it one way and then was left crossed eyed as it spun across him to hit his off stump.

'What happened there?' Compo asked him as they passed each other.

'I have no idea,' Gatt admitted, shaking his head.

Stinger was reprieved by the slightly embarrassed Bristles and stemmed the flow of runs at the other end. The ever-reliable Beaky was facing—the most organised and best prepared player in the team. The first choice of anyone asked 'who is least likely to give his wicket away?' Unfortunately, Beaky was spooked. The importance of what they were playing for had got to him. He wanted the uncertainty to be over, and he was determined that he was the mouse to do it.

Despite the accuracy of Stinger's bowling, Beaky pulled and drove his first two balls. The third, however, was a cunningly concealed slower ball. Beaky drove at it, but mistimed his stroke, and the ball went straight up into the air. Higher and higher it went and then hovered for a moment. At about this time, all the close fielders, wicketkeeper and bowler made their way, at speed, to the point that they judged the ball would land. As the ball returned to earth, the rats came together in a fantastically mistimed collision of fur, arms, legs and tails. The ball finally landed in the middle of it all.

'OUCH!' a single cry went up from the middle of the heap, shortly followed by another.

'How's that?'

At that moment, a moment of intense horror

passed through the onlookers. It was like a shockwave that even the rats could sense. Beaky walked back to the gate to be replaced by Beefy, the scoreboard showing 53 for 4.

'Good Luck, Beefy,' a mouselet cried. 'You can do it!' The others, who'd been silenced by Beaky's dismissal, picked themselves up and joined in with their support.

Beefy's start was a nervy one, and Rags completed the over with two appeals for LBW. In truth, most of the rats didn't understand the LBW law, but nonetheless, they weren't pleased when Bumble turned them down. This had only added to the tension, and as Stinger stepped up to bowl the next over, Bumble stopped him.

'Excuse me, young fellow m'lad, just how many overs d'you reckon on bowling?' Bumble asked.

'As many as it takes,' Stinger replied curtly.

'There's a limit you know,' Bumble pointed out.

Bumble was right, in a normal T20 match each bowler was only allowed to bowl four overs. However, this hadn't been explained to the rats at the start of the match.

'Nobody said anything about overs at the start of the game,' Stinger pleaded, stretching his arms out in exasperation.

'You can't just start making the rules up as you go along because it suits you,' Bristles, who'd muscled in on the argument, added.

With just Compo at his end for support, Bumble became intimidated as the rats clustered around him.

'I g-guess in this instance, we'll have to make an exception,' he stuttered.

'Bumble, you've got to be kidding,' Compo implored. He could see that the game would slip away from them if Bumble gave in to them.

'What can I do?'

Mr Cheese had sauntered over to give his views on the subject.

'As the other adjudicator in all of this, I say that whatever Stinger says goes. Now, can we get on with this, please?'

So Stinger bowled again. It was down to Compo and Beefy now to get the bulk of the runs, and they knew it. With the cream of the batting line up gone, they were the last of the recognised batsmen. With their extra overs, Rags bowling mystery balls, and Stinger having struck his rhythm, the pressure built. The batsmen became becalmed. Beefy's entrance would normally have meant runs, lots of runs in a swashbuckling manner. Instead, both he and Compo negotiated the next four overs only picking up a handful of singles and the odd two.

At last there was a change of bowling with Fleabag brought into the attack. Stinger and the rest of his teammates were pretty certain that this would not end well. However, a bowler who is thought of as being easier or weaker can often undo a batsman, particularly one who's been concentrating hard against difficult bowling. It turned out that Fleabag's bowling was about as sensational as his batting, and he sent down a succession of pea rollers. These weren't difficult to defend, but they were incredibly difficult to score off.

Compo watched Beefy get more and more frustrated from the non-striker's end. It was not a good sign. So when Beefy had three goes at whacking the fourth ball of the over, hitting his own wicket in the process, no one could have been less surprised.

Knotty was a little more happy-go-lucky in his approach. The pea roller gave him an easy first ball to negotiate, and he was able to knock it into a gap for a single. Compo did the same, and the scoreboard was on the move again at 74 for 5.

Having recovered sufficiently to make a contribution, Long Tail came on to bowl. Once again, his outstanding physical attribute wasn't suited to cricket, and his tail flicked off the bails at the non-striker's end.

'NO BALL!' Bumble did the honours.

Then just when his teammates were tut-tutting him, Long Tail came into his own. Compo drove his next ball back up the wicket. It cannoned off Long Tail's tail and ran out poor Knotty, who was backing up and out of his ground. Never can the saying 'Cricket is a cruel game' have been truer.

Thommo was the first of the bowlers to join Compo. He was obviously pretty wound up if his slightly glazed expression was anything to go by. Compo as the 'recognised' batsman would need to try and farm the strike to make sure he faced as many balls as possible.

'I'm not sure where the runs are going to come from,' Don confided in Beefy, who was angrily taking his pads off.

'I'm afraid it's down to Compo now. If I hadn't been such an impatient chump, I'd still be out there with him.'

Beefy wasn't the only player whose impatience had got the better of him. Compo had sent Thommo back when they might have run an easy single. He was keen to keep the strike and hopefully hit a boundary. Thommo had other ideas, and he pressed for one run on the next ball. Compo reluctantly agreed, setting the competitive Aussie mouse up for his first ball. This he duly hoisted into the deep and was caught first ball.

The mouse spectators all groaned and put their heads in their hands. CMJ marked it carefully in his book and showed not the slightest flicker of concern.

Compo gave Ranji a firm talking to about the game plan. All the running should be on his call, and there would be no risk-taking. Ranji was happy to abide by his rules, as Willow had yet to make a bat wide enough to complement Ranji's batting technique. Despite that fact, he managed to nick the first ball he received and a most welcome 4 nudged the score onto 80 for 7.

Stinger now found himself in a quandary. He'd pushed his luck bowling Rags and himself beyond their allotted overs. Spiff was erratic and Bristles a disaster. He'd have to give Fleabag and his pea rollers another over.

Fleabag took the ball and gave it a rub. He'd given

his bowling action some serious thought during the last over and was keen to show some improvement. He ran into the wicket doing a routine that would have gone down well on 'Strictly Come Dancing'. A stuttering, waltzing run up that produced a full toss down the leg-side that Compo helped over the boundary for 6.

The mouse supporters cheered, but they were all aware that there was still a long way to go. The tension was beginning to show in the rats' ranks too.

'Hold up,' Bristles announced, walking into the middle of the wicket. 'You!' he was pointing at Stinger. 'What on earth are you doing using this idiot at this stage of the game?' he gestured towards Fleabag.

'Oi, steady on! I'm doing my best.'

'Either I'm captain and you work with that or you don't.'

'What if I don't?' Bristles gave him a shove.

While the rats squabbled, in the basement something insignificant, but to an old man miraculous, was happening. The final click of the lock's pins had clicked into place, and McCrackers was free.

'Ha ha, I'm a genius' he cried and rubbed his hands in glee.

Bumble had intervened in the rats' argument.

'Let's all calm down, fellas.'

There was still some unhelpful and pointless argy-bargy going on, with Bristles complaining and throwing his weight around. Eventually everyone settled down again. Fleabag bowled, and Compo drove him firmly through the covers for 4.

'Go back to your daisy cutters!' Bristles yelled.

Stinger had to agree it wasn't a bad idea, and the flow of runs was staunched.

Bristles insisted he come back on to bowl, and an intimidating over followed. The mice were able to scramble a run here and there mainly due to the fact that Spotty the wicketkeeper was struggling to stop Bristles' venomous deliveries.

The penultimate over was bowled by Skunky, who'd done well at a moment's notice to contain Compo, who'd given a batting master class. At the end of the over, the match was finely balanced with the mice on 99 for 7. They required 4 to win, with Compo on strike, but Bristles chomping at the bit to bowl the last over.

Chapter Fifteen

Having finally unlocked the door and escaped, McCrackers was keen to seek out some creature comforts. The light filtering in from outside the building was just sufficient to illuminate the portly figure as he made his way up the stairs. At night it was never totally dark in the pavilion. The internal security lighting meant that McCrackers was able to navigate his way to the main lobby without any trouble. He was absolutely starving, and his tummy made a thunderous rumble to remind him of the fact.

During the day the bar that ran parallel to the Long Room was full of little treats. It was probably worth having a mooch around. With any luck, there would be a lonely rock cake under a glass dome. The rotund shadow passed through the door and did a quick tour of the length of the bar. There was nothing obvious on it, but perhaps if he had a little rummage behind it, he might strike lucky. He guiltily lifted the hinged portion of the bar and slipped behind it. By the cash register he found two fingers of a chocolate bar wrapped in foil. It was just what he needed, and he munched on them contentedly. Next to him someone had left a broom propped up against the counter. He grabbed it gratefully to use as an improvised walking stick. He leaned on it heavily and finished his chocolate while reflecting on the evening's events.

In front of him stood the double doors that led into the middle of the Long Room. A line drawn from him would have passed through the doors, across the Long Room and out beyond to the middle of the test wicket. The groundsmen had long since been and covered that after the day's play.

However, there was another wicket that the imaginary line would have bisected too, and that was still very much in use. Not only that, but the improvised floodlighting was creating a curious glow through the glass doors.

Good sense told McCrackers that at this hour he was alone in the building, but the noises coming from behind the door suggested otherwise. He made his way out from behind the bar and pressed his face against the glass.

As a man and boy, McCrackers had watched a good deal of cricket. He'd witnessed all sorts of cricket matches, and many of them from within these walls. Eton vs. Harrow, Army vs. Navy, even teams that had claimed to play 'The Rest of the World'. He'd heard of strange ones such as the 'Men with One Leg' vs. 'Those with One Arm', but he'd never encountered one between rodents. Forgetting his dislike of the breeds of the players on either side, he watched the play in fascination. From what he could see, it looked a reasonable standard. Certainly the mouse batting at one end had a very professional-looking stance. He looked a little out of his depth as in comparison, the bowler he was about to face was a fearsome brute.

As McCrackers watched from the doors and the mouse spectators held their breath, Compo faced Bristles. With four needed to win, he'd have to take whatever runs he could, even if it meant Ranji facing. At least they had wickets in hand.

Stinger had a game plan as well. He'd spread his fielders around the pitch to save runs. He was happy to give Compo a single, but the main thing was to protect the boundaries.

Bristles ran in and bowled the first ball. A yorker right in on Compo's toes. The mouse managed to dig it out, and there was a single for the taking.

'Yes!' Compo cried and the two mice ran.

The next ball to Ranji was short pitched and very

hard to deal with. It was never going to bowl him, but he flailed at it as it sped past him and the score remained on 100. Now sensing an easy victory, Bristles bowled the same ball again to good effect.

Compo beckoned Ranji over to him.

'Three off three now, Ranji. It isn't impossible by any means; just try and get some bat on the next ball.'

Ranji nodded an Indian sideways nod that meant yes, but looked like no.

The ball made its way back to Bristles. He gave it a quick rub, turned, ran in and bowled.

'*SNICK*' Ranji's bat on ball was clearly audible.

'*WHACK*' the ball hit Spotty's gloves.

If there was a way of making a '*CLANG*' sound now, Spotty could have used it as the ball went down. A missed catch, and to add insult to injury, the mice scampered a single.

Bristles snorted with fury. However, if this was the incentive he needed to bowl a dot ball, then it worked, as Compo played at and missed a fast out-swinger.

Another midwicket conference followed, which Bristles interrupted.

'Come on! Get on with it,' he urged.

'Ignore him,' Compo said quietly. 'A single will level

the score, so make sure you back up well, and then run like the wind.'

'I'll do my best,' Ranji replied nervously, clearly feeling the pressure.

Bristles had done well to put his early howlers behind him. He was brimming with confidence as he bowled the last ball. As it arrived Compo, normally such a correct batsman, tried to slog the ball to 'cow corner'. It was a strange rush of blood that ended up with him bottom edging the ball straight down. The ball came to rest just in front of him, having travelled no distance at all.

'RUN, RANJI!' he yelled and set off himself.

After bowling, Bristles had continued his follow through. In a couple of bounds, he was now bearing down on the ball. In a two rodent race, there was only going to be one winner. He got to the ball, picked it up and with a triumphant roar threw it at the stumps.

The mice let out a collective groan as Ranji, still some way down the wicket, had to have been run out.

'He missed!' one of the mouselets squeaked with glee.

Groans changed to cries of 'RUN AGAIN!' as the rats scurried about in an attempt to field Bristles' overthrows.

The damage was done. Bristles' strength, which had seen them through to this point, had backfired on them in the end.

'Nooooo!' Bristles howled and kicked the stumps over.

Ranji, Compo and Bumble met in the middle of the wicket, hugged and danced in a circle.

The mice on the boundary were overjoyed, jumping up and down, hugging each other and whooping with delight. Don and Beefy shook hands, and the other players put their arms round each other's shoulders. CMJ inserted a full stop after the words 'won by three wickets' in his scorebook.

If they thought their troubles were behind them, then the mice were wrong. Bristles was in no mood to take the rats' defeat in a sporting way. In fact, he wasn't going to take the defeat at all.

'ROUND UP THE MALES!' he ordered in an ominous-sounding growl.

There was pandemonium around the improvised cricket pitch as the rats tried to grab the mice. The mice in turn did their best to fight them off. The ladies and children shrieked with despair.

Suddenly a crash stopped them all in their tracks. McCrackers had opened the double doors, bashing them back on their hinges. He stood with his arms flung wide, an impressive silhouette framed in the doorway.

'STOP THAT, YOU NAUGHTY BOYS!' he shouted. It was a funny thing to say, and he wasn't quite sure where it came from, but it had the desired effect. The rats stopped dead in their tracks, and the mice grabbed their opportunity. In an instant, they were off scuttling, scampering, breathlessly dashing for the security of the radiator cover and home.

Don and Beefy ushered them in one after another. Through the long arch under the cover and down through the hole to the safety of their under-floor dwelling.

Up above ground, McCrackers was buying them more time by doing his best to chase the rats around. Whacking at the ground with the broom, they jumped this way and that to avoid him, yowling with fear if any of his shots were too close for comfort.

As the last mouse disappeared, Don and Beefy followed them down. Now they had their work cut out to barricade the way into their home to keep the rats out.

They grabbed anything and everything, passing the objects in a chain from all over the residence. Precious items such as a comb and everyday things like plastic bottle tops. Part of a pencil, some kitchen cloth, leather from a wallet, safety pins and two silver teaspoons. A chunk of wood from a broken bat found in one of the dressing rooms. They used their part-made bats, the stumps from the cricket net, pen lids, strips of napkins and a rusty key. They built a framework that they stuffed with their own bedding. If it came to it, they'd brace themselves against it. Whatever it took, they'd keep the rats out.

Upstairs the rats had had enough. There was only one way out that they knew of, and that was the way they'd come in. While the old man was busy bashing at one of them, then another would take the opportunity to slip down under the radiator cover. Fleabag was one of the first. He stuck his snout into the barricade and was dealt with very efficiently by the front line of workers. He was happy to slip away through the 'thunderbox'. As his tail disappeared, Skunky descended and went straight on through. One by one, the rats swept past in a rush of sleek fur and scampering feet.

McCrackers was exhausted. He perched on one of the long tables and rested as he watched the rats disappear. Bristles was the last of them, and he stopped and looked back at his tormentor.

'Yah Boo, be off with you!' McCrackers called after him, and with that, he disappeared.

Under the floor, Bristles found the mouse barricade. He put his shoulder to it and gave it a half-hearted shove, but all his fight had gone for one night. He gave a final sniff in the direction of the mouse residence and slunk away.

It was time for McCrackers to go home. He pushed himself off the table and did one spin on his heel.

'You're safe, little mice!' he called out and lurched off to find a taxi.

Chapter Sixteen

With the test match over, everyone in the ground had an unexpected extra day in their calendar. Mr Hobbs had an added day to prepare for the next scheduled function, and the mice had a day to get back to normal. Sometime after Bristles had given them his parting shot, a work party had gone out to dismantle the cricket pitch. Whether they had a new ally or not, it was always better to leave no trace of their existence.

Compo's innings had sealed the mouse victory, but it hadn't been one of his best. His unbeaten 21 had earned him a day off chores and provided the mouselets with a new hero to imitate in the nets. As a reward, he'd taken himself up to his vantage point at the top of the building. He was enjoying the breeze and reflecting on the past day's events.

What a lot of upheaval there had been. Even now, Don, Beefy, WG, Beaky, CMJ and Gatt were meeting to discuss how they might make the mouse residence more secure. Their bad experience was a warning that they weren't going to ignore. For now, he'd relax and look forward to the next cricket. He'd only have to wait a day. A one-day match, the club was hosting the

Melbourne Cricket Club. Thommo would be full of himself and insufferable if the Aussies won. *Why not?* he chuckled to himself, Thommo had given his all in their cause. A little friendly rivalry never hurt anyone as long as you were all the same breed.

For Bob, recently retired from Pest Arrest, life was going to be very different. He'd received an immediate response to his emailed application to Hiber Nation. One of their employees had had an accident and their Cornwall Branch was desperately in need of an extra hand. It was an arrangement that suited both Bob and the new organisation, and they'd accepted him on the spot. Bob lived with his sister and her husband, and they were happy to get their spare room back. They'd even lent Bob their van for the journey.

Bob was keen to say goodbye to Stanley and wish him luck for the future. Pest Arrest's clients, however, still needed to be serviced. When he dropped by at the Pest Arrest depot, Stanley had already set out on a job. Bob was given the address, and it was a location he knew well—the disused Royal Mail sorting office.

When he got there, Stanley and his new colleague were just emerging wearing gas masks and coveralls.

'Oi, Boris, look what the cat's dragged in,' Stanley

joked. 'This is my old partner, Bob.'

The two men nodded a greeting.

'Don't let him give you a hard time, Boris. He's power mad.'

'I wouldn't say that,' Stanley replied.

'You did just insist on lighting all the smoke bombs,' Boris said quite seriously.

'Maybe I did, but I'm a highly trained operative, and anyway, you're the new guy,' Stanley paused. 'Okay, I admit it, I've been desperate for Bob to buzz off so I could step into his shoes and be in charge.'

They all laughed.

A group that wasn't laughing was the colony of rats that once again were on the move. They watched the men from the safety of a privet hedge. They had no idea how long they'd have to stay there before the acrid smoke had dispersed.

'What are we going to do, Bristles?' Spiff asked.

'Sit it out. The smoke will clear eventually, and we'll be able to go back.'

The rats were sat in a long line under their hedge. Things were looking pretty miserable for them, and they'd all gone very quiet.

'I was talking to the nice lady mouse...' Spotty

broke in.

'You what?' Bristles spluttered.

'When you were batting, I was talking to the nice lady mouse. She was telling me about the church gardens. There's a big tree with a mossy base that's all hollowed out; she was saying that might be a nice cosy place to live.'

'Outside!' Bristles snorted in disbelief. 'You expect me to live outside?

The rats were silenced as the three men walked past their hedge. They were discussing Bob's journey.

'I've borrowed this from my brother-in-law,' Bob explained.

'What on earth is it?' Stanley asked.

'An old ambulance. It's pretty cool, don't you think?'

'You're not going to camp in it, are you? It's got glass doors.'

'No, I've got lodgings at the sanctuary, but I've got masses of stuff to take down there, and this was the best thing for it.'

'Let's have a look then; I've never been in an ambulance… touch wood,' Stanley said, touching his head.

Bob opened the back doors of the old ambulance.

'The windows would have been blacked out, but my brother-in-law scraped the black film off them. It's quite snug inside now; he goes on fishing trips in it.'

The rats sat tight for what seemed like ages. Eventually, Stanley stepped out of the back of the ambulance.

'I'm very disappointed the siren has been disconnected. It's a pity, you could have done with it. That road down to Cornwall can be a nightmare. A little blast of the blue lights and sirens would get you out of any traffic jam.'

'I don't care what the traffic's like. I'm looking forward to my carefree life in the country, however long it takes to get there.'

As he spoke, there was a sudden honking of horns. A little old lady driving an old Morris Minor had broken down in the middle of the road and was being tooted mercilessly by other London road users.

'Come on, let's give this old duck a push,' Stanley said.

The three men left the ambulance and went over to push the car to the side of the road.

What a lot of upheaval the rats had suffered. They'd lost their tube station home and their friend The

Dodger. They'd believed they'd found a solution to their plight, only to see it slip away from them. As they worried again about what would become of them, an idea of searing brilliance came to Bristles.

'Come on, you lot, we're off to a better life. Everyone in the back of that ambulance, now!' Bristles ordered.

Without argument, the rats bounded out of their hiding place, and one by one hopped up the steps into the back of the ambulance. The inside of the vehicle was full of all sorts of interesting-looking cupboards and drawers. It was as if it had been made for rat transportation.

'Thank you all. That was most kind of you,' the old lady thanked her saviours as they crossed the road and made their way back to the ambulance.

Bob closed the doors.

'That's me off then.'

'Bob, old bean, it was nice to have worked with you, mate.'

'You too, Stanley.' He clapped him on the back. 'Best of luck, Boris, and don't let him boss you around too much.'

With that, Bob jumped in the driver's cab and

started the engine. He gave Stanley a wave and drove away.

His route took him past the Grace Gates and the entrance to Lord's. McCrackers was just getting out of a taxi outside them as Bob drove by.

'Hmm, that's a funny old thing. I haven't seen one like that for years,' he murmured to himself.

He followed its path as it drove past and away from him.

In the back window, Bristles, Spotty, Spiff and Stinger were framed. They gave McCrackers a wave as they left for their new life, but he'd turned away. He had something very urgent to discuss with Mr Hobbs.

The End